
Acknowledgments

"The Sun Will Rise" is embedded with true events and stories. Although, the character names are fictional, for the sake of safety, all stories are still completely nonfictional. The israeli-Palestinian conflict is an issue we are all completely aware of but our interest towards it has been decreasing as there are no updates: people are just dying and a country is just under constant siege.

This is a reminder to everyone who has forgotten the issue: just because we haven't been talking about it like before, doesn't mean the conflict has eased or stopped. As human beings, it is our responsibility to help our brothers and sisters.

One day, the sun will rise and Palestine will be free. No one will be exiled from their land, starving and or living under siege but until then, help us help our brothers in any way possible.

You'd think an explosion is loud, and it is. It just doesn't feel as loud as you'd imagine and ironically, the worst part of an explosion is the vacancy that follows it. "Am I the only one who's alive?" was the first thought that came to my mind that night. The explosion was so loud that the pain in my ears was what had actually woken me up and not the loudness itself. I opened my eyes to a battle scene; the room that I had lived in since the day that I was born was unrecognizable to my own eyes. The roof had collapsed and shattered all around me, the windows and doors were broken; an easier way to describe what I had just witnessed would be by simply just saying that every single thing in the room was shattered into small pieces. Every single thing in the room, including me and my fragile heart. I was twelve years old when I learned the definition of true heartache. It is not the moment your best friend walks away or the guy you love no longer loves you; it is the moment where everything you have ever known breaks into shreds and all you can do is sit helplessly and witness your world shatter around you. I understood what heartache truly is when I was twelve years old... the day I opened my eyes to see my house destroyed and my family members officially announced as martyrs. Despite the tragedy though, this was still just a typical day in my one and only occupied Palestine.

I was unable to process my own thoughts. I went completely blank. The paramedics rushed into the house, carefully making their way to my physically limp body.

"What's your name?", one of the paramedics asked. He was a middle aged man who was taller than anyone I've ever seen before. He looked at me with his warm eyes. "My name is Yousif, what's yours?"

"La... Layal," I was now at a loss of words.

"Are you okay?"

I nodded my head. I was numb. I didn't know if I was okay or not. I just wanted to go to bed and wake up believing that all of this was just a nightmare. It didn't really happen. It couldn't have really happened. I'm not really all alone. Am I?

"Do you understand what has happened?" he slowly asked.

I nodded again. For god's sake can he stop asking me questions already.

"Do you see my friends over there?", he pointed to his right where three women were standing quietly looking at us. They all gave off the same energy; warmth. "They'll take you to a place to live with girls your own age who you can play with, okay?" I could tell he was trying as hard as he could to show me some sort of positivity but all his efforts were useless because I just lost my entire family and nothing could ever bring me happiness after that. My grandparents, my parents, my elder brother and my five-year-old sister, all gone. I nodded again. At that point, if I hadn't said my name earlier then he'd probably thought I was mute. I followed the three ladies into a car. They tried to make conversation all throughout the car ride but my mind was somewhere else. I couldn't comprehend what had just happened. This has got to be just another nightmare. I have never felt this downhearted in my life and I am sure I never will but I couldn't even cry. I always thought that your tears are a measure of how sad you are but I was wrong. My heart crumbled and shriveled in my chest but the only thing I felt was numb. I could not let out a single tear. I slowly felt myself drift away into another world; a world where I could have possibly felt happy, even if for a little while.

One second of happiness and my brain starts replaying everything in my head. I scream. I can't get it out of my head. Why can't I get it out of my head?! I feel someone's arms around me, "you're okay… you're safe," the social worker whispers into my ears. I ease back down into my chair and try to sleep but the nightmares just won't let me. Oh Palestine, I love you with every drop of blood in my body, why would you take away everyone and everything that I love? I turned my head the other way and looked at my beautiful country. Sheer beauty; no matter how destroyed it is. My mind raced with thoughts at one mile an hour and I was unable to grasp everything that was going through my head; I thought and thought and thought until I physically exhausted myself and closed my eyes and drifted away.

My eyes popped wide open, the sun has now been replaced with the moon. The moon had always represented my mother to me because just like her, it constantly brightened up this dark and dull world I live in. I was probably as young as 5 months old when I first witnessed someone die in front of me and you'd think that living in a country where people are killed on a daily basis would in a way make you feel immune to pain. It doesn't. Every time we see or hear about someone's death, it hurts the exact same way it did the first time. You never get over death, even if you encounter it a million times.

"Where are we going?", I asked the social worker. I've been in this car for almost a whole day but my brain didn't even bother to wonder where I was being taken. I felt out of this world; I was physically there, however; I was mentally with my family, in heaven. I always imagined what heaven looked like… I hope it's as exquisite as they describe it to be. I'm not happy but at least I hope that they are.

"We're going to a home where you'll be able to play with many girls your age," she tried to be as positive as possible in such situation.

I wondered if those girls have been through what I have just been through. I really hoped not but my situation is as common as divorce is. It's a fairly normal thing to go through where I live.

"Are we nearby" I asked, starting to get sick of this never-ending road trip.

"Ten more minutes," she said, she wrapped her arms around me again and started caressing my hair, "how are you feeling?", she asked.

"I'm okay," I quickly answered, without even thinking about it. Obviously, I was not okay but there was nothing to say anymore. I could not get myself to stop thinking. My chest felt heavy and I was completely and utterly numb. In a way, although I had literally just seen my family's dead bodies right in front of me, I was still unable to grasp what had just happened. I sat in silence in the car for the next ten minutes and I was not the kind of person that found silence calming, silent moments always just seemed awkward to me but right now, after hearing a bomb go off; this silence was very comforting. It felt peaceful in a way, it made me feel like there still is hope for everything to get better. The car made an abrupt stop. My heart dropped. I looked out the window only to see men in israeli military uniforms.

I lost control of myself. "You killed my family! You killed my entire family! May you rot in hell!", I shouted completely unaware of my words. The social worker held me close, "shh......", she whispered over and over again.

The soldier aggressively opened the car's door, "stay quiet or I'll kill you as well," he said threateningly. He raised his gun into my face. "What did you say again?", he asked challenging me. I was about to shout again until the social worker held my arm, reminding me that I am in a life or death situation. I eased back into my seat and remained quiet. "I thought so," he mumbled, "stay out of trouble little girl," he threatened and carefully lowered his gun and closed the car's door as hard as it was humanly possible. He allowed our driver to make his way through and we continued the painfully long car ride for another fifteen minutes. "We're here," the social worker excitedly said. I personally was not excited and didn't even know there was anything to be excited about.

Chapter 2

My feet felt like bricks as I dragged them across the road into a building. The building was painted pink. How cliché. I never really understood the point of assigning colours to genders, I reminisced of the days where I was younger and had a pink room when in reality, my favorite color was blue. But blue was a "boy's" color so I was stuck in the pink room whilst my brother had a blue room. I wondered if he felt the same way. The thing with the Arab world is that there is a drastic change between what it means to be a man and what it means to be a woman. Never in my life did I ever witness my mom have a job or be passionate about something whereas my dad had a career to pursue and dreams to accomplish. It always saddened me that I would one day have to grow up to an empty life; a life where I was allowed no education and no dreams. With heavy steps, I made my way down the corridor; the corridor had inspirational quotes on the walls and pictures of girls who were brought into this house at a young age and later were able to make something of themselves… as sad as I was, that gave me a glimmer of hope. Sometimes we don't realize how important these little things are… I normally wouldn't have given this sort of thing any kind of attention but although we don't realize this, we are never hopeless; we are always subconsciously searching for a speck of hope somewhere. And my glimmer of hope was a poster that said "the sun will rise", as simple as that.

"This one's your room," the social worker interrupted my train of thought, "if you need anything, you can find me or other members of the staff down the hall," I nodded my head and she continued to introduce me to the other girls in the room. I had three roommates but sharing a room wasn't a new thing to me, I had always shared a room with my sister. My family came from an entirely low social class; some nights I went to bed hungry because we couldn't even afford food. Despite how crowded our dwarfish house was, I loved it. I didn't realize that until I had literally lost my house. The social worker left the room and I straight away laid down on my bed.

"Are you okay?", asked my roommate, Fairooz. She looked about my age, maybe a year older. Her hair, in contrast to mine, was so blonde that it almost looked white and her eyes were a shade I had never seen before… they weren't blue or green but rather somewhere in between… I'd go as far as to say they were turquoise but she had little specks of grey within her iris; in a rather beautiful way, her eyes literally felt like a gateway into her soul. They looked really pure, as if she has never seen a death in her life. I later found out that she was spending some time playing dolls with her baby sister near her front door when a bullet shot her sister straight in the heart. She died from the impact straight away. The same night, israeli soldiers tore down her house as they violently made their way into her house and forcefully took her father to a police station where they pressured him into saying he killed an israeli soldier, although he didn't do it, he wished he did. He was burned with cigarettes and beaten down brutally until he lost his life. He was then thrown right in front of his house to be a lesson to all those who aspired to retaliate against the israeli government. Fairooz woke up one day to go ride her bike when she saw her father's body, stained with blood and bruised so bad that she hardly recognized him. Her scream sent her mother straight out of the house and the minute she saw her husband's disfigured body, she lost her mind. She didn't sleep, talk or eat for weeks. She wasn't even able to feed or take care of her daughter and when the relief program found them, they admitted her mother to mental health facility and they took her to this shelter. She hasn't seen her mother ever since. After she finished telling me her story, her tears had already made their way down her cheeks. Fairooz's story was three years old yet she still talked about it like it was yesterday so it made me think; will I ever be able to get over this?

"Trust me though, this shelter will actually start feeling like home sooner than you realize… Look at Ayaa and Maryam over there," she pointed at the bed on the other side of the room and continued, "they truly are my sisters so don't worry… it does get better." I hope so, I thought to myself.

After Fairooz had walked back to her part of the room, I laid down on my bed and decided to go to sleep… maybe when I wake up, it would really be a better day. My mind drifted back to my family but now I felt as though I was over the phase of disbelief and into the part where I actually start to miss them. I missed them so much and there was utterly no worse feeling than missing someone but not being able to do anything about it. The family photograph I often looked at before I went to bed had now turned into a silhouette in this unfamiliar house I was stuck in. My aching heart was preoccupied with a pain that would often come and go but was more excruciating in these quiet moments. I wish I knew how regretful the death of a loved one would make me feel… at least then, I would have tried to spend much more time with them. Sleep pooled on my eye lids, and the noise around me started to slowly fade until I heard nothing at all. I saw nothing at all. And for a couple of hours, I was nothing at all.

I awaken suddenly, my thoughts in high definition and my veins pumped with adrenaline. I immediately get out of bed. I hear voices but my brain cannot comprehend what's going on. Soldiers in the middle of my room. A gun straight to my head. My roommates, in tears, screaming at the top of their lungs. I rub my eyes. Am I dreaming? I try to move or cry or do anything but every single normal body movement in my body has subconsciously been put on hold. I felt as if I was breathing as hard as I possibly could but no air was entering my lungs. My whole world had paused for an eternity. I felt a hand on my arm as I was violently dragged into a car by one of the israeli soldiers. It's funny how the human brain works; in a moment of extreme fear, I had lost my ability to think clearly and logically. I was yanked by my arm and forcefully put into a car with five israeli soldiers, one of them constantly pointing his gun at my head. The soldiers spat at me, cursed me and threatened me but the only thing that I could think about was that they hadn't given me a chance to brush my teeth or change my clothes. How embarrassing. I looked down at to what I was wearing: a white shirt and navy blue shorts. Streaks of fresh red stains covered my thighs. Without realizing it, I screamed as loud as it was humanly possible. I saw the bullet in my thigh before I even heard the gunshot or even saw the soldier shoot. I screamed once more and a white cloth was now put into my mouth. "If you scream one more time, I'm shooting you straight in the head," the soldier said as his eyes widened, his previously pale face had now turned red and I could physically look at his veins pop out on his forehead. His blood was boiling so much that he was literally in a sweat. I remained quiet but my thoughts started racing. I was confused. What happened? Why did I wake up with a gun to my head? Why did they only take me? Where is everyone else? My eyes started watering and the tears made their way out and I no longer had control. I felt a kind of loneliness I had never felt before… I was on the thread of death and there was literally no one to save me. The windows of the car were sealed and I couldn't see anything; I didn't know where I was or who I was with. I just knew that this could very likely be the last car ride of my life. I listened to the soldiers speak in Hebrew but I had no idea what they were saying. My parents always bugged me about learning Hebrew, they said it would be helpful in situations where I had to deal with israeli soldiers, I just never expected to have to deal with israeli soldiers at this age so I never learned the language. This was the day I regretted not learning Hebrew if at least I understood, I would have been able to understand what they were saying to each other. They could have actually been speaking about me and I would have figured out what exactly was going on but I had no idea of anything. I just remained quiet the entire car ride… afraid that today was going to be the last day of my life.

Chapter 3

The car came to a sudden stop and before I could even come to grasp what was going on, I was aggressively pulled out of the car by my arm. I instantly screamed in pain. My feet landed on the ground and I could feel the sores start to develop on the skin of my bare foot as I suddenly landed onto a non-asphalted road. I landed exactly on top of a sharp rock. I could feel my foot starting to bleed on impact. I felt restrained as I could literally feel something holding my arms; it felt like a round metal object holding my wrist in a steady position. Handcuffs? Did they really just handcuff a child?! I tried to resist, I moved my body in a jerking motion but I decided to stop when I realized that the more I move, the more it will hurt. I could no longer feel my tears as they made their way down my cheeks. I wanted to wipe my tears but I could not move my hands. My hands were literally tied. "Are you scared?" asked the israeli soldier mockingly as he dragged my limp body across the street into a police station. The white and blue flag was raised everywhere and stitched on the uniforms of the soldiers who had me in custody. As soon as I saw that imaginary country's flag, my blood started boiling. I felt overheated and the nerve on my forehead popped. I could not control myself, my body shook uncontrollably like an animal who has just been set loose after years of living in a cage; I had a rage within me that had to either be released or held within me until it killed me. This was just the beginning of a revolution; my revolution! My dad used to always tell me that anger was the friend of the devil and in this situation, israel is the devil so there was no way that I'd let my anger get the best of me because I would have most likely ruined any chance I had of getting out of here and being a revolutionary. My picture and fingerprints were taken and I was quickly processed and became an official prisoner. At the age of 12. After THEY have brutally murdered my entire family. How ironic. Oh, and what was my crime? Creating terror by threatening police officers. I actually was confused… didn't they terrorize me when they bombed my entire house? When I watched my only home break down and all my family members die? Don't they terrorize me on a daily basis when they bomb my country and I have to wake up to a war every day? When they killed the children of my beloved country? When they occupied my land?! They teared my whole life apart but I guess I'm the terrorist. Two prison guards carried me; one by each arm and then they literally threw me… not in a cell though, in solitary confinement! Because apparently I was a high risk prisoner and I was too dangerous to be put with other people. They said I would create chaos if put with others. It wouldn't be safe to the other criminals. I was 12 years old!

Solitary confinement was exactly how I had imagined it to be. A small room with no windows and no outlook into the world. The walls were plain white and the door was made of stainless steel. White tiles covered the floor and the best way to describe the room was by saying that it was a plain, dark room. And just like the room, I had reached the darkest point of my life. I sat cross legged in the corner of the room and rested my head on the hard wall behind me. What happens from now on? How long will I be put here? Am I ever getting out? I didn't know the answers to any of those questions. I sat in the darkness and pondered about my life. I just didn't understand the whole israeli-Palestinian conflict… this is my country. I was born here. My siblings and all my descendants were born here. So why didn't they have the right to live here as well? Why did they have to die? I laid down on the cold floor and looked at the ceiling above me. I felt like I was trapped. Oh wait, I was actually trapped. Just then, a soldier opened the door in front of me. I absorbed as much light as I possibly could. "This is dinner," he said coldly as he handed me a small cup of soup and left. The portion of soup was not even fulfilling to a two-year-old but I drank it anyway and went back to laying down on the tiled floor. I closed my tired eyes and went to sleep, not sure if I even want to wake up the next day.

Sadly, though, I did wake up and I wish I hadn't. I tried to move my fingers only to realize that I am completely numb. I was freezing to death. Was that some sort of sick way to torture me? Yes, it was. I curled myself in a ball on the floor, trying so hard to warm myself up but all my attempts were utterly useless. Footsteps could be heard from the other side of the doors and so, I started screaming at the top of my lungs until the door flung wide open. "Shut up!" shouted the soldier. He was wearing a coat so thick that the coat itself looked double my weight and was still visibly shivering.

"Please turn the air conditioner off. Please," I begged the soldier.

"I can't do that," he quickly said.

"Can you at least answer one question?" I asked.

He nodded.

"What have I don't to be put here? Criminals belong in jails… I'm not a criminal."

"You need to learn to ask less questions," he dismissed my question as he left and closed the door behind him. A couple of minutes later, I noticed that the temperature was getting warmer. I was finally able to move my fingers. I sat cross legged in the corner of the room. My life has turned into nothing but a series of misfortunate events. My mom always told me to look for the light at the end of the tunnel whenever I'm feeling down and I always did, but today, I am incapable of looking for that light; metaphorically and physically. The room I was imprisoned in had no lights, it was literally just a dark space surrounded by four plain walls. I tried to think of a future I could look forward to but at that moment, it felt like I had no future. And even if I did have a future, what could it possibly be? I lost my loved ones, I lost the only place I could call home and I was stopped from continuing my education. What future would I possibly have? I gave up. My dad always told me that giving up is not in our blood; we are fighters and we go through everything together as a family and so, I guess he was right. We are fighters but only when we go through the hard times with our family and I had no family. Have you ever experienced a life where you actually didn't have anyone to talk to? I have and I could tell you there was no worse feeling. I had a best friend back home, Noor, she was often the light at the end of the tunnel but I haven't seen her since the incident. I wonder if she's safe back home. Noor was a girl from another universe. She was my age but I saw life in her eyes; her eyes always glimmered with hope and I have never seen her frown in the seven years of our friendship. Noor was also my neighbor so we often played in the streets or rather whatever was left from the streets that were bombed by those I'm imprisoned by. We witnessed our first death together. Noor also lost her brother, Yousif. He was only sixteen years of age when he passed away. I still remember him so vividly; just like her, he had those hopeful eyes. He used to come out and play with us whenever he could. One day, when I was in their house, the israeli forces attacked their house and took him for interrogations. He just never came back. He was presumed dead after disappearing for five years. At first, I refused to believe that he could have really died but holding on to him was toxic. I woke up every day waiting to see his cheerful face. He always made me laugh, I never expected him to be the reason I was upset. I unconsciously sank onto the floor as I thought about Yousif. Was I gonna be another Yousif? Or what if I ended up seeing Yousif when I'm out of solitary confinement. I don't think so but there's no harm in hoping. The door was opened again, a piece of bread was put on my floor and the door was just as quickly closed. I leaned over, took a hold of the bread and leaned back onto the wall. The hunger I was feeling was overwhelming. Without even thinking about it, I put the dry bread into my mouth and swallowed it straight away. I was far from satisfied but it felt so much more fulfilling than last night's soup. I paced around the room for hours trying to calm my nerves down until I realized that all this pacing is going to make me hungry again and so, I stopped and sat back down in my humble little corner of misery. Sleep has always been my escape from this cruel world but being this hungry, sleep was nowhere close to me. It was only first full day in prison but I had already felt like I have grown twenty years older. You'd be surprised as to how many thoughts can come across your mind when you have nothing else to do. My mind drifted away from the problems in my own country and I started thinking about other countries, countries that are trying to overthrow their own governments. Are they aware that there is no such thing as complete equality or justice? In my opinion, revolutions are unnecessary and useless because they, in no way, create a complete change in the social and governmental system. All a revolution does is move the pain from one sect of the country to another. I don't know if you're completely understanding my point so let me try to clarify it more to you. In most cases, abusers have often been abused as kids; they carry around all this negative energy for years and then when given authority, when they have grown older, they release this energy in the form of abusing others whether it be their partner or their children. Although, it is not supposed to happen, it still is a normal cycle of life. So, when citizens of a country have been holding on to so much negative energy for years, being the underdogs and dealing with social injustice, the minute they get the opportunity to do so, there is an extremely high chance of them snapping and abusing their power too, in a way, seek revenge. All the so called 'revolutionary' is going to do is move from one extreme to another. So you're probably wondering, if revolutions are useless then what should we do when facing injustice? Accept it? Absolutely not! The ONLY way to get over social injustice and create a better society, although easier said than done, is it make steady but slow changes from within your ruling government. That is how you make things better and not ultimately worse. I started thinking about all those countries that are wasting their time doing something that will not even better their society or country in the long term. I sighed. At this world. And at myself. I suddenly remembered my cousin Ammar, who was killed last year. It's funny how everyone I've ever known was either imprisoned or killed, including myself. Ammar was 12 years old when he was killed, he was so young and my family members always said that losing someone so young is more tragic than losing someone who is older in age. I beg to differ. I don't think age has an input to how much death can affect the victim's loved ones. I have lost people who were infants, children, teenagers, adults and elders and I can conclude with confidence that it all hurts the same way. Sometimes though, when older people die it's even more tragic than the death of children. Losing Yousif was harder on me than losing Ammar. Yousif showed promise. He showed perseverance. I always saw Yousif as someone who was able to free Palestine one day, he was very determined and was actively engaged in society. Yousif was the hope I saw in the world and so I lost hope the day I lost him. I remember the day Ammar was killed like it was yesterday. It happened in my own house. We were playing outside when we saw israeli soldiers going completely insane with their machine guns so we ran quickly into the house to find safety. Ammar was standing next to our window when a bullet smoothly made its way through the wooden window and into his forehead, it penetrated his brain and the massive bleed killed him straight away. I remember the screams the second his body hit the ground. I lost my ability to talk or walk, I literally just froze. I saw my dad and uncles try to first aid him although they knew he was already dead. That was the only time I've seen my father cry; Ammar was like a son to him. He spent most days in our house and only ever went home to sleep. He was a part of us that we will always miss. We lost and missed a lot of people and they will all always be in our hearts forever. I closed my eyes to reminisce on all the good memories I had with Ammar and found myself finally falling asleep.

Chapter 4

It's just another day in solitary confinement and I am slowly coming to believe that torture inflicts less pain than this. Being put alone in a dark room is slowly driving me crazy. All I'm left to do is think and think and think and there's a certain point at which thinking becomes too much to bear. The door remotely opens, a tray is pushed inside and the door is directly closed. The door was sealed so heavily because you know, I was a dangerous prisoner. It was almost as if I was the one who bombed a house and killed people, not them. I pulled the tray towards me too see a bowl; it looked weird. The bowl had some sort of yellow liquid inside of it, for a split second I thought it was soup then I recognized the smell: urine. They had just literally served me a bowl of urine. I pushed the tray back towards the door, laid down in the corner and poured my entire heart out in the form of tears. I was starving. Whenever I visited my friend's house, I noticed that their fridge was full of food whilst ours wasn't. We often just had bread and yoghurt and I would complain so much when I got back home, my parents must have gotten sick of me. I never realized how blessed I was to at least have something to eat until it was far too late. A couple of minutes later, the sealed door was opened again and a soldier was standing behind it. The soldier had some sort of warm vibe that I didn't understand. He didn't talk at all, he just dragged me from my arm and threw me in a prison cell. Where I had roommates. Thank god. I was a minor and I knew there were special prisons for minors however, I was in between all ages. The officer locked the cell and walked away. The other prisoners were all shouting curse words at him. They were all filled with rage and so was I. So I cursed too. The prison quieted down as he left. I made my way to my bed and sat down, feeling a little bit more safe than I did in solitary confinement. Time has taken away the beauty my roommate once surely had, she was a woman of old age; she had short white hair and a wrinkled face but I could tell that in her time, she turned heads when she walked into a room. "Is it your first day?" she asked.

"No… I was in solitary confinement," I said as I swallowed my words, "for three days."

"Oh, most of us have. I've been here for the past 35 years."

I was now able to see the weird mixture of sadness and hope in her eyes.

"What happened?"

I listened to her story intensely. At 4 AM, she heard a knock on her house's door and immediately came to the conclusion that the israeli forces were there to demolish her house since they had a received a demolishing order a couple of days ago. The officer said he had an arrest warrant for a someone called Khalid. None of her family members were called Khalid but when her father said that to the officer, his face turned red and it felt like his blood had started boiling. He asked them to name every person in the house and if he refused to do so then tear gas will be thrown into the house so her father complied. When he reached to her name, the officer asked him to stop and told him that his daughter has been throwing rocks at the officers. They immediately marched into her room and handcuffed her without even giving her a chance to change her clothes or wash her face. They dragged her into a van. There were about 20 israelis in the form of police and special forces in front of her house. They interrogated her for 24 hours, not allowing her to sleep and electroshocking her every time she accidentally fell asleep. They wanted her to admit that she had thrown stones but she looked away and refused to answer. The officer then put out his cigarette in her eyes and constantly gave orders for the other police officers to hurt her. She was pushed against the wall and physically abused until her nose bled. She then admitted that she had thrown rocks because they told her that once she confesses, she would be free to go home. But she didn't come home and was still in the same place 35 years later. I admired her strength as she told her story, I was still unable to physically state what had happened to me because every time I tried to, I would immediately break down and lose my ability to speak. She pointed at one of the guards, "he was one of the officers who made me bleed… I still vividly remember everything although it was 35 years ago," she said with anger pulsating down her spine. She asked me what my story was but I just told her I was not ready to talk about it yet; I just didn't know what I did to deserve all of this. She only replied with three words, "God is great." And God, indeed is great and I knew he'd help me out of this.

To say that I hate Jews is an overstatement. I don't hate Jews. I hate Zionists and not all Jews are Zionists. A Zionist is someone who supports the religious-political movement of creating a homeland in the Holy Land of Palestine or as they like to refer to it, the great fictional country called israel. I strongly believe that we, in no way possible, have the right to point fingers and judge other religions because in the end, all religions in one or another have one goal which is to spread peace. Anyone who does anything other than that is going beyond their religion. I can't blame all Jews for the israeli movement just as I don't expect them to blame me for the ISIS movement. I had Jewish neighbors before my house was bombed and they were the most warm hearted people I've ever met. I loved them! Heck, I still love them. I remember I once had a heart to heart with their daughter, Chava. Chava was about two years older than me and she had actually learned how to speak Arabic and always considered herself as an immigrant. She always said that this land was not a property of the Muslims or the Jews, it was just the land of God and we were guests on this land.

The stars used to cover the sky above us and we'd lay down and look at them in awe as we spoke. She introduced me to the concept of Zionism and how it was a different ideology from Judaism. She constantly told me how her Jewish family have never believed in the Zionist movement. Isn't it weird? Our religion is the most important thing in our character, it is what makes us who are, it lays down our morals and principals and yet, most of us, did not choose our own religion. We were born into a family and had to believe their beliefs and if we ever had any questions that were remotely out of the box, we'd be accused of being Atheists. That was what Chava told me when I once innocently asked her why she 'chose' to be a Jew. Despite our differences in race and religion, Chava was one of the few people who had a big impact on my life. She taught me right from wrong and was always here for me regardless of all our differences. I really hope she's doing well. My roommate's story also reminded me of my best friend, Noor. Noor had also received a demolishment warning a couple of days before my incident. I wonder if they had demolished her house yet but most importantly, I wonder if she's safe. I stopped for a second and prayed: Dear God, please protect my best friend and her family from harm.

"Are you alright?" asked my roommate, interrupting my train of thought. I nodded and jumped from the chair I was sitting on and climbed the stairs to my bed which was on top of her bed. I really needed a change of clothes. Or maybe just a shower… but the israeli officers had turned electricity and water off. According to my roommate, they do that every once in a while for a couple of days to try and tire us so we wouldn't complain and make a fuss about everything else that is wrong. I was slowly starting to lose my hair… stress I guess. It has been around 24 hours since I've last had something to eat, despite being hungry, I still felt disgusted because of the urine they gave me in the morning that I couldn't make myself eat. I talked to my roommate about that and she said that they had once forced her to drink the urine and she still has nightmares about it at night. They held her by both arms and forced her mouth open while they poured the urine in. She was shaking as she told me the story. I could tell she will probably never get over the experiences she went through here. I felt lucky that although I've been imprisoned, I still haven't been physically abused. I really wished that I would be out of here and will not end up like my roommate. I wondered if any of my friends have tried to contact me in the last couple of days and do they miss me in school? I hope they haven't forgotten me. Everyone is probably at school now. I still can't believe I'm here. The day passed as fast as my thoughts raced in my mind. I finally fell asleep.

Chapter 5

Tear gas had bombarded the house, I was running for my life, literally. It felt like there was no way out; I was running and running but just didn't seem to reach anywhere in particular. I was wheezing and was incapable of breathing properly. All this tear gas was too much for my asthmatic lungs. I collapsed. The house is now being hit with israeli artillery shells and live ammunition. I tried to cover my head with my arms as much as I could but it was of no use. Live ammunition had made its way into my ribcage and to my heart. I gasp and jolt up. It's just a nightmare. "Are you okay?" asked my cellmate who I later found out was called Hanan. I told her about my nightmare and she assured me that we are somewhat safer than how we were back home and it's all going to be okay. It was really ironic how we are safer in prison than we are at our own homes, I mean yes, some of us did get abused a lot but it was still much better than being bombarded by bombs in a way… alright, it was not better, we were just less likely to actually die.

Hanan told me about how she used to have a lot of nightmares when she first got arrested but now things are feeling more acceptable in a way. Hanan was the epitome of Hanan, warm-heartedness, in my life in prison. I climbed down from my bunk bed and sat on the floor facing her bed. "Do things actually get better or do you just get used to it?" I asked.

"Do you want an honest answer or just an answer that will make you feel better?"

"An honest answer," I said, hoping I'd still get an answer that will make me feel better.

She looked at the floor, "it doesn't get better and you never get used to it. I feel at ease knowing that the younger generations are willing to work to free our country as many of them have been on the news or even arrested nowadays. I feel pride when I see that despite everything that we suffer from, us, Palestinians, still manage to fight back and I promise you, Layal. We will break free as long as we have a bold and brave generation like you." I felt like she had given me more credit as to what I was in the Palestinian community. I wish I was bold or brave or whatever but I only felt broken. After I lost all the people who I loved, what else was I supposed to feel? My heart suddenly felt heavy. I haven't had a day of peace in this country but yet I still loved it with every piece of my heart. Your country will always mean something special to you even if it has been hard on you, that's just how it is. "Try to go back to sleep love," Hanan lovingly said, "good night." I wished her good night and climbed back to my bed. I laid down and mumbled the national anthem to myself:

بحق القسم تحت ظل العلم

بأرضي وشعبي ونار الألم

سأحيا فدائي وأمضي فدائي إلى ان تعود

And this was the night that I vowed to do everything I possibly can to free my country from the israeli occupation, even if it meant sacrificing myself in the process. This was my cause and I was willing to die for it. The night went on in an unexpected way, for the first time, I was unable to sleep. Insomnia had made its way into my eyes as I was filled with fire. A fire within me was burning to revolt. I stayed up all nights brainstorming plans as to what I should do to help my country; should I start a food strike? Should I pick fights with the guards? Should I start a protest from within the prison? I thought of a lot of different possibilities as to what I could possibly do but then came to one realization. Any act of defiance within the prison was only going to get me killed before I even got the word out. And so, I decided to wait. I decided that the best plan was to first get out of here and then make a global and local change within the community, that was the only way I could actually make some kind of difference, even if minor, in my Palestine.

The sun had probably risen but sadly, I haven't seen the sun in days. I was starting to get familiar with the darkness and dullness of this place. I jumped off my bunk bed to a piece of bread. Finally. Some proper food. I ate as if I haven't eaten in years; like someone who has been denied from something for so long and then finally gets it. Hanan stared at me as I ate in an undomesticated manner and then offered to give me her piece of bread but I refused; she was probably just as hungry as I was, if not more. She insisted but I also insisted otherwise. The guard came to our cell and opened the door, ordering us to start social work, we walked along a long mundane hallway as we made our way to the prison's court where there was a garden. We were then instructed to plant trees. I was unsure if trees would actually grow in a wicked place such as this one. Although plants and animals are not scientifically as smart as we are, I always believed they have a way to connect with mother nature; in the end, they actually were a part of mother nature. I took a shovel and starting digging whilst Hanan and the other inmates did the same. We were working in some sort of unison and I could tell we were all thinking the same exact thing: why is the prison so concerned about plants when it literally has more important problems to deal with. It felt like around 150 degrees and the sun was starting to drain all my energy. It was hot. I was drenched in sweat, completely dizzy and weak. I tried to stop but the guards immediately threatened to hurt me. I continued to work under the horrid conditions and the unbearable heat until we were ordered to stop, three long hours later. As soon as we had stopped working, the officers sprayed boiling hot water on us, claiming that this was some sort of shower that we were supposed to enjoy. The color of my arms had slowly started turning into a pinkish red, they had burned my skin. I didn't know if the guard had a heart or not as I witnessed him laughing intensely at the amount of pain we were in. I just didn't understand why we were being treated like convicted felons when in reality, most of us have been taken in as inmates due to faults of the own israeli soldiers or even false, manipulated confessions of things we didn't do. The israeli soldiers were the real criminals; they were thieves! They stole my right of getting an education, they stole Hanan's right of marrying someone and starting her own family, they stole Noor's right of spending her childhood with her only brother and most importantly, they stole my family's right of life. They should be accountable for all the damage they had done in my country. They killed, tortured and stole. But we were the ones who were in prison. I was later told by Hanan that I had a right of attorney but although I would try to fight the system and get out, there was 95% chance that the judge would rule in the favor of the israeli government. That is, if they even allowed to get the case to court. My feet heavily made their way into my prison cell. My prison cell was a really small room; it barely fit a bunk bed and a small urinal. The walls were the palest shade of white I've ever seen and the side of the bed that was behind my bed, had some writings on it. "Free Palestine" was written over and over again on the wall and a small sketch of the Palestinian flag was present. I thought that it must have been Hanan or hopefully a former inmate who is now free; the later gave me some sort of comfort and hope. All I seemed to be looking for lately was a glimmer hope. Despite my many efforts to find some kind of hope, I always seemed to fail. I mean I could easily trick myself into believing that there is hope but the harsh reality of it all was, I was unsure of everything and nothing in particular. Although my life was agonizing, the years seemed to pass by like seconds. I don't know if I felt older because of my experiences or because I had actually grown much older in a span of what felt like five days but was in reality, five years. It was a slap in the face to in fact be in the same place five years later. Hanan had started losing her strength. I woke up in the middle of the night one night, only to see her drenched in a cold sweat. She stopped sleeping and had lost her ability to move as swiftly as she used to before. Although, she was in desperate need of health care and support, the israeli officers denied her the right of healthcare. Just another right they've stolen from us.

Chapter 6

It was my 17th birthday when I was finally a free citizen – or as free of a citizen as it gets when you're in Palestine. My first breath of fresh air swiftly made its way to my lung; I took in a deep breath and for the first time in years, I felt at ease. Feeling at ease was not something familiar to me, even before everything had happened, I was always agitated, worrying about the next israeli move. In a way, I felt like I had already experienced the worst so could it possible get any worse? The only way left to go was up I guess. I made my first steps of freedom to nowhere in particular; it just hit me that I had nowhere to go. Was I truly alone in this big scary world? For a second I even thought that prison might have been better than the real world. I walked aimlessly but somehow ended up in the same shelter I was taken to when my family were killed. I walked through the familiar corridors until I found one of the volunteers. "Layal?" she was in a state of shock. I couldn't believe she actually remembered me; I literally only stayed there for one night before being forcefully taken to prison and humiliated. I nodded. "I was in…" I tried to explain but she quickly cut me off. "I know," she said and so I decided not to talk about my life in prison.

"I don't have a place to stay," I said, unsure of why I was here and why I was telling her everything.

"We can give you a place here but since you've been arrested before, I think it's better for us to help you move into another country as an asylum seeker."

Despite all the hardships I've faced, something poked my heart. I didn't want to leave. A country is something so divine and the love I carried for mine was beyond describable. My country has hurt me in every single aspect of my life; I've lived here all my life and every day had its own hardships but I didn't want to leave. To love a country is to feel an emotion that is different to everything else and I love my country. I would die for my country.

"Do I have too?" I asked, in horrid terror of leaving.

"You don't have too but it is much more safe, they can arrest you again at any time, I highly recommend leaving."

"Where to?" I asked.

"Sweden or Norway would be your best two options."

I took a deep breath, "let's do it then."

The next words that came out of her mouth were inaudible to me. I couldn't believe that I was leaving this country. This is the country that I was born in, raised in, and to this day, I have never left it before. I nodded completely unaware of what she was saying. Apparently we were leaving tomorrow, she was going to get my files ready tonight and file me as an emergency case and drop me off at the airport tomorrow. I was anxious about the idea of flying in a plane, it was one of the many things I've never done before. I was so limited to specific areas in my country that I couldn't even imagine what I would see there or how my life would be like. I was just told that I had to leave if I didn't want to get into prison again and I really didn't want that. The last five years were the hardest years of my life; I forgot what sunlight was, I forgot the idea of a world outside the four walls I was stuck in. Hanan made everything bearable but it never got any better than bearable. I wasn't tortured as much as the other inmates but just seeing how much they were in pain and the suffer and mental turmoil they went through was more than enough to make my heart sink on a daily basis. My heart had sunk so many times in the past five years that at this point, I literally felt like my heart was laying on the floor. It was stepped on and was in an agonizing amount of pain; just like me. If I didn't have Hanan by my side, I would have probably even forgotten how it felt like to be a human being or even feel anything at all. The importance of having a good support system was made clear to me in the lock down, there were many times where I would suddenly lose my patience and turn completely numb but my cellmate always shook me out of it; she made sure I'd never turn into the numb soulless people who are often created after years of prison. The volunteer assigned me a room at the other side of the corridor we were in. The room was next to the volunteers' rooms and was a spacious room just for me. I felt at peace. "If you need anything at any time, I'm in the room next to you," she said kindly. I thanked her and closed the door behind her, finally getting some alone time for myself. I mean yes, I did love Hanan and enjoyed spending time with her but sometimes you just want to be alone. I tried to mentally prepare myself to a different world outside of my dear Palestine but I still vowed to keep fighting for my country even if I am a million miles away. I settled into my room and lit up one of the candles on my bedside table; I fell asleep as a I watched the candle stick burn into nonexistence.

The sun had risen and I was already on my way to the airport. The volunteer dropped me near the airport entrance but I had to make my way alone all the way to Norway. israeli officials stopped me near the gate and examined me, making sure that I don't have anything dangerous or illegal with me. I didn't know if everyone just kept treating me like a criminal or if this was the actual procedure of travelling; I've never travelled before. I checked in.

"Don't you have any bags?", asked the airline employee.

I nodded in a 'no' motion. The employee was in complete shock seeing that I've got a one-way flight to Norway with no luggage at all but I actually didn't have anything to take with me. This is what happens when you spend five years in prison. When you go through so much, you start losing the grasp of what is weird and what isn't, I hadn't realized that it was an odd thing to travel without luggage. My house was bombed and so all my clothes were gone. I stayed in the same clothes until the next day where I was imprisoned. In prison, we were given navy green clothes to wear; it was like a uniform and we had to wear it every day so the concept of dressing up was long forgotten to me. After I was let out of prison, I was given a pair of jeans and a white t-shirt because the clothes I was detained with could no longer fit me and so, I wore the jeans and shirt to the airport today. It was the only pair of clothing I had. I took my passport and flight ticket and got lost amongst the crowd of people walking all over the place. My head started spinning, I was completely unaware of where I should go or what I should do. I passed through passport control and into the departures lounge. At this point, I had no idea what I was doing, I just followed the crowd of people and ended up near my gate. My ticket said Gate 5A but my flight was after three hours and so, I took a sit in front of the glass wall that overlooked my beautiful country. From the glass, I could see the Aqsa Mosque's from afar and so, I stopped for a second and prayed that one day, I'll be back here when my country is free of this messed up occupation. I sank in my seat as I came to the realization that I won't see this view, possibly for the rest of my life. I haven't seen this view in years but it felt like I did every single day; the beauty of Palestine was, is and will always be engraved in the depths of my heart. The concept of having a country is a bizarre yet beautiful thing. I was born here and I always thought that I would've died here but fate had a different plan set out for me, I am indirectly being forced out of my country and I think this is what they do to revolutionaries here; they throw us in prison or force us out of our own country. They probably thought that I would forget my country once I settle in somewhere else, what they didn't know however, was that I had already vowed to spend the rest of my life supporting and helping my Palestine. My plane had started boarding and so, I entered the airplane and made it to my seat. I expected to feel a bit more at ease when I'm seated in the airplane but I was even more anxious. I was leaving and it was sinking in my brain, and my heart did the same. Okay, I'm on my way to Norway now but what happens when I reach there? The volunteer gave me a phone number and an address before I left, she instructed me to call the number when I land and inform them of who I am and where I'm from and they were supposed to help me until I could settle down by myself. A boy around my age sat down on the seat next to me. I hate being around people. You'd think spending time in prison made me want to meet people and put myself out there but all it did was make me more anxious and more afraid of people. I had this irrational fear that everyone out there wanted to harm me and even if they did help me, then they probably want something back. I often debated if acts of kindness could possibly have absolutely no selfish motives behind them. I mean, we do everything with some sort of selfish motive. For example, Hanan helped me when I was in prison, probably because she wanted to feel good about herself or she wanted to feel what it's like having someone to take care of knowing that she will never be a parent. Our friends talk to us to fulfill their own social needs. Our friends play with us to entertain their selves. It is human nature to want to seek your own happiness in anything that you do. There is no such thing as a pure act of kindness. The simplest selfish motive that is embedded in every single act of kindness is probably the feel good factor. I heard a loud noise and the airplane started shaking. I grasped the hand rest next to me as hard as I could and closed my eyes. Apparently, the airplane took off.

"First time flying?" asked the boy seated next to me. I nodded. "Me too," he added and I stayed quiet.

I wasn't interested in any form of small talk; I was frightened to death of what the future was holding for me. Most people would prefer to talk about it when they're feeling frightened or anxious but I am one of those few people who'd prefer to just remain quiet. I think it's a weak characteristic to talk to others about your fears, it just gives me them the right to use your weaknesses against you. I always carried myself by myself and walked with my head held high; I religiously refused to show any sign of fear. I had nine more hours to go before I landed and had to actually deal with the anxiety I was feeling deep inside. I had to settle by myself at the age of 17, keeping into consideration that I had a very limited education. I had the right to be panic-stricken.

"Asylum?" I heard the guy next to me ask. I nodded. I limited talking as much as I could because I didn't want to engage in any sort of small talk but he insisted to talk. I guess he was bored and so was I.

"Talking helps time pass," he said and for the first time I turned my head to look at him. His dark brown hair was a contrast to the color of his eyes; they were a beautiful light blue. He had freckles all around his nose which gave him a very approachable look. "I'm Mohammed," he said with a warm smile.

"Layal," I replied. His warm eyes spoke to me more than anything ever has; maybe I haven't felt like anyone cared about me up until now. "Are you seeking asylum too?" I asked, genuinely hoping he's landing in New Zealand for asylum just like me. Maybe then I wouldn't have to be so alone; we could've sorted the whole asylum thing together. What was I thinking?! I've literally just met this person!

"Yes, I'm moving to Oslo and I've got absolutely no idea where to go or what to do after I land. My father is a political figure and so, I am at high risk of imprisonment. The lawyer just thought it was better for my wellbeing to live abroad. I lost my mom years ago to the israeli occupation. She was a politician too and was killed in prison. She was tortured so much that I didn't even recognize her body when I saw her in the morgue…" his voice started breaking and my heart broke too as I saw the pain in his aquamarine eyes that were brighter than the sun itself. It's weird how much empathy you gain when you've experienced the worse. I just seem to naturally feel everything every other person around me is feeling; I feel connected to the world around me and the issues I'm surrounded by. It is ridiculous. You'd think I'd be immune to pain at this point but the only thing that happened was that I was able to feel even more pain than I'd used to before. I was more aware, I'd say. I knew exactly what he was talking about.

"Why Oslo?" I asked in an attempt to change the topic and make him forget the pain he reminisced on in that second.

I don't know really… I had two options: Australia or Norway. Australia just seemed worlds away so I chose a closer country just in case that one day, it'd be easier to go back." He was hopeful, just like me. His life is a privileged life in comparison to us all. Although his parents suffered, he never did. I know it's painful to lose parents, trust me, but it is a million times harder to watch as you lose them. He stopped my chain of thoughts as he spoke, "so what's your story? Why asylum?".

"I was in prison for the past few years; I didn't do anything. They didn't even tell me why I was arrested. I just woke up one days with guns pointing at my face. It was the most terrifying experience of my life. I was set free yesterday but I was told that there is a very high chance I'd be arrested again or even worse, attacked. So I just have to move. I've never been to Norway before, or anywhere in that sense, but I have no other option. Either I move or I risk losing my life and I'd think I'd be more useful alive than dead." His warm eyes penetrated itself into my heart. No. He was starting to pity me and there's nothing I hate more than that. "Don't look at me like that, I'm not just another sad story," I snapped. His face turned pale and he apologized at a pace of 20 times per second. I assured him that it's okay and apologized myself for snapping at him. It was a normal human reaction and I shouldn't have snapped. I guess I was just scared. I've been scared a lot for the past hour. I can't believe it's been an hour already. He was being more resistant to speak; I think I scared him. It is absurd how we are put into this world only to deal with so many problems; some people can handle it but other can't. Before I went to prison, one of my close friends killed herself. What she did was very frowned upon and I remember people in the neighborhood talking about her for months. Despite the fact that what she did was a sin; she was mentally ill and couldn't take it anymore. I always wonder if God would forgive her; everyone says he won't but what if she committed suicide when she was having a depressive episode? What if she did it when she was unaware of her actions and incapable of thinking straight? God says that when a person is sick, they are excused of certain obligations. She was sick. Maybe not physically but she was indeed, mentally ill. I really hope that God would forgive her for what she did. I knew her. She wasn't the kind of person who'd just end their own life. I mean, I wasn't there when it happened, I don't know what happened but I do know that she was not aware of neither her actions or her thoughts the moment she did it. The airplane suddenly staggered like a drunken man and I held tight to my hand rest. Did I run away to get safety and just end up dying on the airplane? Mohammed looked at me with a reassuring smile. I looked back at him and saw ocean waves in his blue eyes; waves always calmed me down. And so did he, in an unfamiliar way. At that moment, I thanked God that he was with me. Usually, in moments of need, we subconsciously cling on to the people who make us feel safe; our family, but I didn't have a family anymore so in a moment of need, I seemed to cling on to the first person who'd give me any bit of attention. The TV monitor in front of me flickered from time to time so I had learned to just ignore it but an alert suddenly appeared on my screen. My eyes laid on the monitor and every word I read stung and only fueled the fire that burned inside of me. Every violated phrase was like gasoline to it, my fists began to clench and my jaw rooted and just like that, I was like a middle school science fair project, I exploded like a model volcano. My veins contracted and my face turned to a bright red; I started jerking my hands up and down, trying to focus on anything to calm myself down and not cause a scene in the middle of the airplane. Mohammed's hands made their way on to the palm of my hand, his warmth radiated all the way into my spine and eased me in a foreign away. I felt like someone who has been abolished from their country and was just settling down in a place they could call home. It felt like finding safety in a world of destruction. I know culturally, the guy is supposed to make the first move but all I knew was that I couldn't have possibly let this feeling of safety leave and so I asked him to never leave me. "You know I'm just a stranger right? I could be a murderer," he smirked and my shy eyes made their way to the floor. What have I just done? Why did I always feel the urge to defy cultural and societal norms? In a way, I've always had a theory that we will always seek to do the things that we know we're not allowed to do it. knowing that something is not acceptable, just sparks a light in us humans and urges us to try it. I just seem to want to try everything first hand before deciding whether it's acceptable or not. My theory though, is also statistically approved. I mean, don't you see it? It is often countries where alcohol is banned that the consumption of alcohol increases. It is countries where free speech is not allowed that are revolutionary. As human beings, knowing we can't do something, only tempts us to do it. "I won't leave you," he suddenly said. His soothing voice was music to my ears; it echoed to my heart and I felt drunkenly euphoric every time he spoke. "You can't get mad every time you read biased news, you and I both know what this whole israeli-Palestinian conflict is about, we don't need the news to tell us about it." He had a point. We are leaving to a Scandinavian country, we are for a fact, going to meet people who are Pro-israel and I can't let my blood boil every single time. Seeing fabricated news about your country on the television is the most frustrating thing in the world. I just didn't understand how those who come up with those fake news had the conscious to spread a negative image of such peaceful citizens. The news stated that Palestinian teens were engaging in harmful acts towards 'innocent' israeli soldiers. First of all, they are in no way possible innocent. Second of all, what do they expect? Seriously? When your country is being occupied and your own people are being killed before your eyes, what would you? It's not like you'll go and thank the soldiers for ruining your life. The concept of media is a very blurry concept to me; I don't and will never understand how people use media to fuel their own propaganda. How can you be so materialistic? Working in the media sector is a noble job and it honestly saddens me how people have taken this job and used it in an unethical way.

Wait what?! Did he just say that he's not going to leave me? What does that even mean? My life is a not a fairy tale, trust me, if I end up leaving with this guy, he's actually going to turn out to be a murderer; that's just how bad my luck is!

"You know what I find weird?" he asked.

"What?"

"Despite everything you've been through, I see a sort of spark in your eyes. I see hope and that's something I haven't seen or felt in a really long time. Do you think moving to another country will actually make our lives better in a way?"

"I hope so… I don't understand what the concept of hope is… Sometimes I feel like I'm living in a make believe. I force myself to believe that life is better on the other side just to be able to hold on. My life is not a typical one… I spent the gap between childhood and adulthood in prison. It was a blur… I subconsciously deleted that part of my life and I don't want to remember it ever again." He looked at me intensely as I spoke as if he wasn't actually listening but rather just trying to make sense of the way my lips moved in order to understand what I was saying. His eyes glimmered with a feeling that I couldn't come to fathom. "Do you believe in hope?" I asked him and cut off his gaze. He looked at me like I was a physics equation and he was trying to solve me.

"I do… as unexpected as that is. I believe I can build a life there. I believe in hope, in the sense that, I believe I can be partially happy but I don't believe in hope in the sense that we will one day be free. Sadly, the world is all about money and israel is able to pay off governments much better than we'll ever be and so, as long as it pays, it will have international support. I do believe that before the day of judgement, God will take our right, our land, from them but I don't believe that we will. In the end the whole policy of the world is in the hands of our worldwide leaders and sadly, our leaders choose to turn a blind eye to our case because to them, it is nothing but a waste of money and resources."

Although, I was tricking myself into believing that I was hopeful, his words really put me down. From the minute we started talking, this was the first time he had upset me. I felt the glimmer of hope in my eyes fade and my smile drop into a frown. He was right and I knew it. My false hope shredded to pieces. Even though what he said upset me, his view was a very logical and practical one. I respected him for it and admired him for looking at the world in a reasonable way and not being afraid to state his opinion. He talked with confidence and immediately stated his point. He didn't beat around the bush when he spoke, unlike everyone else that I knew. In a way, he seemed so familiar yet so foreign to me.

Finally, at ease, I had a couple of hours of sleep until I was woken up by the pilot announcing that we were about to commence landing. Just like me, my anxiety also woke up from its slumber and started shriveling in my chest. What was I supposed to do now? Despite how afraid I was of flying, the flying part of this whole journey was the easiest part.

"So, when we land… are you coming with me?" asked Mohammed, carefully weighing his words.

"I don't know," I replied. I didn't know anything at that moment. I remember as a kid, my mom always told me not to talk to strangers and he was a stranger that nonetheless, I felt so at ease with him. But could have I possibly left with him? I don't think so. We were about to land and I had to slowly come to a decision. I looked at him and then took a paper and looked at the number that I was supposed to call as soon as I landed. He handed me a piece of paper and said, "just in case you change your mind." The paper had an address on it, probably the place where he was staying. I liked his company but he was not my type of person. He actually was privileged; he was staying in a villa whilst I had to stay in a shelter. My mind was racing as I was trying to decide whether or not to leave with him. I mean, he was a stranger but so were the people in the shelter I was going to. After my family were all killed, everyone was a stranger so how bad could it be? Although it was completely unreasonable for me to leave with him, I was subconsciously trying to justify it to myself. The engine started whirling as the airplane made a steady landing. The landing was either so much smoother than the take-off or I had just gotten used to it. The seatbelt sign was turned off and I unbuckled my seatbelt. I was about to get up from my seat when Mohammed called my name.

"Layal," he said and I looked back at him, "can't I at least drop you off to wherever you're going?" he asked.

As I said before, fear always makes us cling on to any person who is available to support us. "Okay," I said, "let's go."

He got up from his seat and followed me into the airport. We walked side by side through passport control, I watched him get his luggage, we got into a taxi and left, in complete silence. There were a lot of words that hanged in the midst of this silent atmosphere, mostly words of me confessing that I really wanted to leave with him. The silence felt like a comfortable lullaby and my brain was in another world; a world where it was acceptable for me to lean on him for support although I don't know him that well. I snapped out of it and called the number I was given. A woman answered; she sounded really young and sweet. She gave me an address and I told the taxi exactly where to go.

"Layal," he softly said. I looked at his ocean blue eyes once again.

"Are you sure that the people you're staying with are going to keep you safe?", his concern was so genuine that I could feel it in his voice.

"It's a shelter. I will be completely fine."

He was trying to make me second guess the whole idea of living in a shelter. I just remembered that the last time I slept in a shelter, I woke up in a prison cell. The devil was starting to make me feel uneasy and afraid. I came to this shelter because the police are unable to get ahold of me here. I am safe. I will be safe. I didn't realize how bad my hands were shaking until Mohammed mentioned it, "I didn't mean to scare you," he said, "I just wanted to know if you actually know those people."

"I don't even know you," I snapped at him. I didn't mean to snap at him but I was nervous and frightened to death and he was absolutely not helping; all he seemed to do was water the plant of fear that was growing in the depths of my heart. I felt my chest go tight and I knew that if I didn't calm myself down in the next few minutes, I will burst into tears. Didn't I just say that he made me feel at ease? What happened? At this moment, it literally felt like he was the reason for all my fears and doubts.

"I'm sorry," he quickly said as he ran his fingers through his silky dark hair. His hair was almost as dark as my thoughts were as I was in a foreign country with a stranger, on my way to somewhere where I literally don't know anyone. Oh and Oslo? It was a complete contrast to where I come from. Oslo was colorful, it was bright; I could feel the happiness of all the people who drove or walked by. Everyone seemed to be happy and carefree. Whereas in my country, we're often stressing about whether or not we're going to wake up the next day. It is really unfair that there is no balance in this world; there are countries that are the epitome of happiness and hope and there are other countries that have only seen destruction and war. Despite the happy vibes that I felt in Oslo, I knew that when given the chance, I would return back to my country in a heartbeat. Nothing can take away the place of home from your heart, even when your home has literally been taken away; it will always be in your heart and your mind. We reached our destination and the shelter looked a million times more presentable than the shelter I was in back when I was a child. I want to say that the shelter looked safe but the country as a whole gave me a sense of safety I had never felt before. I was euphoric and depressed in the exact same time. I didn't even know how that was possible. The taxi's doors opened as Mohammed and I both made our way into the building. Mohammed followed me like a security guard and I was grateful that he didn't leave because despite feeling a sense of safety from the country itself, I was pretty sure that most of that feeling came from Mohammed's presence. "I think you'll be okay," he said. He kind off sounded disappointed; I guess he wanted the shelter to look messy and dangerous so that I'd leave with him but I was in reality, it was as safe as it could possibly be. The shelter had two securities next to the gate as most of the people that lived there were asylums just like me. It was a maximum security building and I was certain that it was safer than Mohammed's house but I still felt uneasy letting him go. Although I felt uneasy, I knew I had to let him go. I said goodbye but my gaze refused to look away from his ocean blue eyes. "If you change your mind, you know where to find me," he said and that itself, gave me some sort of peace. But would I really call him? I don't think so. I mean, yes, he did make me feel safe but in the end, I had to come to terms with the fact that he's just someone that I met in the airplane. Everything felt like a fairy tale and fairy tales don't happen when you live in a war zone.

Chapter 7

I walked away from him and into the large building. I was greeted by a mixture of Palestinian, Syrian and even, Norwegian volunteers. "Welcome to our shelter, here we provide everything from food to shelter to education... if you need anything, just ask and we will be happy to assist you with love." I was led to where my room was; I had a room all to myself. I stepped into the room to be greeted with a warm feeling; the hardwood floor was a contrast to the light beige walls. One wall had a wallpaper that found its way into my heart. The wall paper had a quote on it that said: one day, the sun will rise. Under the quote, there was a painting a sunrise. It spread all kinds of warmth and hope in my heart. The room was air conditioned although in comparison to Palestine, the weather had a refreshing coldness in it. I felt comfortable. I had a cabinet which was completely useless as I had no clothes but the shelter was nice enough to provide me with another pair of jeans and a couple of t-shirts until I got myself going. To the right of the cabinet was a single bed which had a bright pink covered bedsheet. The stereotypical choice of pinkish colours in the room got on my nerves for a second but then I stopped and just thanked god for providing me with such an opportunity. I was one of the lucky ones. My room only had a small bathroom in it; it almost felt like I was in a hotel. I laid down on my freshly made bed and subconsciously, wondered about Mohammed; where was he and what was he doing? I hope he's safe and as comfortable as I am. Should I call him? No. That's enough. I don't live in a fairy tale. I was starting to get hungry so I made my way to the big hall next to the rooms. Around four girls were sitting in the middle of the room having a pizza. "Layal?" I heard my name and looked at the girls, "Don't you recognize me?" asked the girl, in a sort of disappointment. "No, sorry," I said, "I'm new here."

"I'm Fairooz," she said, very pleased to see me, "you haven't aged a day!"

I suddenly remembered who she was! She was with me in the shelter back in Palestine. I didn't realize who she was because she looked even more beautiful than she did before. Her tired eyes were no longer tired; she genuinely looked happy, I could see it in her beautiful exquisite turquoise eyes. In contrast to the first time, she looked clean and like someone who was actually alive and not just living. She offered me a piece of pizza that I took and started talking to me about all the beautiful things that happened to her since she moved here two years ago. Apparently after the police attacked the shelter and took me, the shelter temporarily closed, Fairooz was moved into another shelter right across town where she got into a fight with a Zionist woman who resided next to the shelter. The woman then informed the police and so the shelter shipped her off here before they could arrest her or get her into trouble. She then continued her education here and graduated with a high school diploma; she had just now gotten into an architecture program in one the universities nearby. I was very proud of the unbelievable improvements in her life and gained a sense of hope that I too, can fulfill what my destiny has entitled me to do. Fairooz introduced me to the other girls sitting in the halls; she seemed to have formed many friendships and was very close to all the girls in the shelter. Fairooz was a lively person, even in the old shelter, she was the one who approached me. She also used to consider our old roommates as her literal sisters. I remembered our old roommates and asked Fairooz about them. She told me that Maryam is in Geneva, she has decided she wants to major in journalism to try and publish unbiased news and raise awareness to the injustice that is happening in Palestine. Maryam had also gotten engaged to an Australian guy she met in her university. Ayaa though, was still in Palestine. Ayaa was arrested by the israeli police during a raid on the shelter one year ago and, just like me, she was put into solitary confinement but that was as fair as anyone knew about her. Ayaa was one of the youngest people in the shelter so knowing what she was experiencing right now really wrenched my heart. I felt heavy as if I was carrying the weight of the world on my shoulders and my world went a little bit darker when I realized just how cruel this world is. I started feeling down but quickly cut off my own thoughts and changed them into thinking of a plan of what I want to do. My dad always told me that the only way we can help our country is by being educated which is why I decided to go back to school and get my high school diploma and then apply to one the universities in the city. I now had a plan but implementing it was a different story; I decided to go to sleep and start working on everything when I wake up the next day.

Sleep came to my eyes easily that night. I guess this is what happens when you finally feel safe. I was no longer afraid to sleep and not wake up the next day or wake up in a prison cell; I knew that I was as safe as it gets. I woke up hours later to the sunlight beaming through my glass window. My eyes slowly opened up to a world that was still cruel but at least had a lot of hope in it.

Breakfast was served in the common area and although I lived in a shelter, I felt like I was royalty. As I had my breakfast, I engaged in a conversation with one of the volunteers about my future in here.

"I'm thinking of continuing my education," I told her.

"That's the most common path of the people in the shelter here and I recommend it as well. There are two options: either you continue your education or get a basic job. Obviously, the first option will lead to a brighter future and a more fulfilling career. We have a school 20 minutes from here which is specialized in the education of those of older ages so, if you want, I'll take you to the school and get you registered and your next plan of university will be discussed later on," I nodded and she continued talking, "you need to understand one thing though, the path you're taking is the harder path, you need to commit time and hard work."

"I'm willing to commit anything it takes, I really want to do this," I said.

"Okay then, we'll leave in an hour. We have another refugee who'll come along with us as she wants to continue her education too."

I continued to eat my breakfast and listened to the girls talking around the table. I loved that it was a mixture of people from somewhat similar background yet, they all ended up doing different things. Most of the people had university degrees; some of them worked in banks, some were engineers, some worked in social work, some were even doctors. I was impressed of the paths they have chosen and achieved and I hoped that I too would be able to reach my goal. I heard stories about girls that finished their university degrees, worked, got married and had their own families. They had started a life that was more comfortable in nature. I wanted to pursue futures like theirs, live my own life but I also wanted one more thing; I wanted to pursue a career that could help my Palestine because that was the most important thing in my life and I was never going to let that cause go. I finished my breakfast and went to get ready to register in school; my first step to be of use to my country.

I heard a knock on my room's door, "are you ready?" the volunteer asked. I immediately opened the door and followed her into a car, I was so excited to start this new journey in my life. The other girl was already there; she was a girl that looked a bit older than me. She had a pale face that contrasted her dark features; it almost felt like she carried a cloud of sadness with her. She didn't look Palestinian, she did look Arab, just not Palestinian. She remained quiet and didn't talk much for the whole car ride, I just assumed that she had a lot going on in her head, that was just the vibe she gave off. I however, continued to engage in small talk with the volunteer. This is what happens when you've lacked communication for a while; I just wanted to talk. I felt like my heart was heavy with words that I have kept unsaid and no matter how much I talked, it never seemed to be enough. My curiosity grew and grew as I watched her distinct hand movements; I was interested in the way she carried herself. Although she was physically thin, her movement seemed to be very heavy. "How are you?" I asked her and watched her gaze dart into mine. She looked at me with some sort of bewilderment, "are you okay?" I continued asking.

"I'm fine," she quickly stated as if she was fleeing from something. The social worker poked my hand, gesturing me to not pressure the girl into talking and I complied to her gesture because she knew best. "So, did you go to school back home?" the social worker asked me, trying to shift my attention from the girl in the backseat.

"Yes I did but not much, I was a kid when everything happened. I can read and write well enough and I'm familiar with basic math but that's pretty much it," I was talking to the social but my mind was fixated on the girl sitting behind me. Why did she act like she was in complete danger although we were well taken care of here? I didn't understand why she was acting the way she was and why the social worker didn't want me to speak to her much. The social worker continued rambling about everything in her life but I had zoned out when she started talking about her childhood and when I zoned back in, she was already talking about her husband and I had no idea what she had said in between all of that. We finally arrived at the school and I followed the social worker into the admissions office. I was given a form that I quickly filled up as I watched the girl fill up her form. Apparently she was Syrian... I knew Syria also had some issues but I didn't know exactly what was going in because I never really watched the news. I didn't believe in the concept of getting news from the media; the media was all biased and the last thing I needed was biased news. I was talking as if I had access to the news... we had no electricity most days! The lack of electricity had cut us off from the real word. I knew nothing about the outside. I suddenly remembered the pro-israeli biased news I saw in the airplane and my blood boiled again. I then remembered Mohammed and everything became still; the world was at peace again. I think Mohammed said something about graduating school already so I knew there was no chance of me seeing him here; he had probably enrolled in a university already. I handed the social worker my paper and was scheduled a test to pinpoint my exact level. I didn't know what level I'd be at but I already knew that it wasn't going to be a high one. The social worker advised me to study for the exam, she said that the higher my grade is going to be, the quicker I would be able to graduate and I wanted to graduate as quick as possible. I had some hope that if I graduated quickly then I could enroll in the same university Mohammed's in before he graduates and gets his degree. My whole life seemed to revolve around him although I didn't talk to him ever since I went to the shelter. In a way, I felt like he was the right shelter for me; I felt safer in his presence than I did in the shelter or anywhere else in particular. We finished the admission process and were both scheduled an admission test. The social worker took care of the rest of the paper work and administration work. My admission test was a week from now and I had already started to get nervous. I used to be one of those students that put a lot of effort in their work and always ended up with the highest grades. I had high levels of anxiety during school days because I truly did stress unnecessarily so much so the anxiety I now felt was very familiar to me. In a weird way, I felt comfort in this sort of anxiety; it felt like home. How cruel could your land be that you'd associate it with the feeling of anxiety? The best part of my life back home was going to school; not to study of course but to spend time with my friends... that used to be the best part until I realized that every day I went to school, the amount of students in my class decreased. Students used to disappear! As a child, I always thought the students no longer came to class because they finally convinced their parents as to why they hate school. I wished that my parents would also let me skip school. I tasted the bitterness they tasted the day my parents passed away and I lost everything I had and could no longer go to school. I now came to wonder about all my friends who suddenly disappeared. Did their parents die too? Or even worse, did they die as well? Thoughts of melancholy invaded my tired brain; I could no longer calm myself down. Every time I think about all the people in my country who are likely to experience what I experienced, I reach the lowest of the lows. This is a form of sadness that is just utterly inconsolable. The social worker looked at me with a look that I have become familiar with; it was pity. The most familiar look of them all, and I hated it.

"What happened?" she slowly asked me.

"Nothing," I mumbled. But even the girl in the backseat knew that it wasn't nothing; I was an excessively talkative and jolly person which is why it was very easy to spot when waves of sadness have hit me and today, it was not just a wave; I was hit by a tsunami of sadness. Should I let all these feelings drown me or fight back? I honestly didn't know. I remained quiet and juggled all these thoughts in my head. I thought about every child who is in an israeli prison right now. I thought of every person who was now experiencing what it is like to get their house bombed and demolished. I thought of every person who is now losing a person close to them. I closed my eyes and wished that I would never be able to open them again but unfortunately, when the social worker touched my hand, my eyes jolted wide open and I knew that I wasn't dead. This was the first time since everything happened that I had actually wanted to be dead. I could always handle pain when it occurred to me but the thought of knowing that there are so many people out there who are in an immense amount of pain right now just downright saddened me. My heart felt like it had the weight of the world piled up on it and I quickly started feeling like the air in the car was not enough; I was suffocating. I rolled down my window and started taking deep fresh breaths of air. It was heart wrenching that back in Palestine, children didn't even have fresh air; a simple human right given to us by nature. Even that was taken away from us. The social worker tightened her grasp on my arm, "it's okay," she said, "I'm here, all the volunteers are here... you're not alone." I knew I wasn't alone. I wasn't worried about myself. I was worried about the millions of children out there who were actually alone with nowhere to go. Social workers saved me when my house was bombed but not everyone gets saved. Its physically impossible to save every single person in the country, I knew that but that still didn't make it okay. Do I just have to accept that some people could get trapped in whatever is left from their house and die a slow painful death? Do I have to accept that children will get taken away and killed? Do I have to accept that people are just going to die? I will never accept such thing because it will never be okay. Is this how dead we have become as humans? We are no longer shaken by tragic deaths! If death doesn't shake or move us, then what will?

My feet felt as heavy as concrete as I tried to drag myself out of the car and into my room. My burdensome body collapsed on the bed. I closed my eyes and just as I was about to take everything in, I heard a knock at my door. "Yes?" I asked, completely annoyed. Some people may want people physically by their side when they're feeling down but I wasn't one of those people. In moments of weakness, I like to be alone. Maybe it was because I didn't like it when people saw me at my weakest points; I liked to portray myself as a very strong person and carry myself with pride in front of others… it was almost as if the way I acted influenced my way of thinking and I'd actually start seeing myself as a very strong person. I was bothered by knowing that whoever was at the door, I had to face them while I was in an extensive stage of self-doubt and misery. The door opened and a volunteer appeared at the door, she was not the one who was with me in the car but seemed to have known that there was something wrong. She made her way into the chair in front of me as if she owned the place. My gaze fixated on the way her movements made it clear that she was filled with an electric feeling of joy. In a foreign way, I could almost feel the joy that she carried around with her. She gave me a warm smile and began to speak, "I heard about your sudden mood swing in the car, I know how hard it is to settle into a new place; this must be a very anxious experience… I understand that, change is one of the hardest thing for the mind and body to get accustomed to and it is completely fine."

Why was she rambling on like she knew what was going on in my brain when everything she was saying was in fact complete and utter bullshit. Okay let me calm myself down and think clearly. What she was saying wasn't complete and utter bullshit, it was completely true and relatable to some people but it was nonsense in relation to how I was feeling. The change was the easiest thing for me to get accustomed it. It's a good thing that I'm not under the constant threat of being arrested or bombed. I didn't hate the change. It was a good change. I would have loved it if I could have stayed in my country and been safe in the same time but that option was not realistic so this was the next best option. "It's not the change I'm worried about," I said, I took a second to contemplate whether or not I should continue talking, "I got anxious thinking about all the people back in Palestine who will never get this opportunity."

Her eyes grew warm but what I saw in her eyes this time wasn't pity, it was something much more than that. Her eyes glowed the way a child's eyes glow at the sight of ice cream. What I saw in her eyes was beautiful; it was hope. I have never seen someone have so much faith in me.

"I haven't seen refugees that think about others in a long time," she took a pause and continued, "I'm very happy to see this in someone but right now is not the time to be thinking about others, now is the time to think solely about yourself."

"How can I think about myself when there are people out there who are in pain?" I interrupted her.

"You can't do anything to help others if you don't help yourself first. Imagine focusing on what you can't do right now rather than working to be able to make an actual change in society, you'll get sick of it! You'll get too depressed to work and you'll literally make yourself sick and when you become sick, you'll be of no use to others."

I started to understand her point but to stop thinking is easier said than done. I didn't expect to feel better but I kind off did. I felt like there is a purpose in my existence. Yes, I knew that I was luckier than the people who were back in my country but I also knew that I could use my privilege to make things better for people back home.

"After you finish your education, come see me and I promise to get you into social work if you want," she said as she made her way out of my room, the exact same way she did when she came in.

I had a lot of things spinning around my head but my mind was also clearer than it was before. I had a path and I just had to make my way through the path and reach my goal. My goal may have seemed far-fetched to some people but the volunteer showed me that it's achievable. I just need to focus on myself for the mean time. I went to the dining room to have dinner and it was not a surprise to see Fairooz there; it was as if she lived in the dining room. I told her about my conversation with the volunteer and she told me how that volunteer is the career advisor in the shelter and she was the one who also encouraged Fairooz to get into architecture when she found out about her interest in sketching. She filled me with more hope when she told me that that volunteer sticks to her word and is known for leading people to special career paths. I ate dinner as I continued to engage in small talk with Fairooz. She told me about her day in the university and talked about the things she learned; she was so interested that her eyes gave a glimmer of joy as she spoke, she also was unable to slow down her speech as she was so excited talking about a sketch of a building she was working on. I was filled with a warm feeling of joy and pride for her; I felt like she had truly found her passion and I prayed that one day, I will too. There was a visible difference as to how she was back in Palestine and how she's been in the new shelter and that difference fulfilled my need for reassurance. Although I felt safe, deep inside, I never knew if I had truly made the right choice by moving to another country.

With a sense of unfamiliar euphoria, I wished Fairooz a good night and went to bed.

Chapter 8

I turned over and over again on my bed as if my constant movement would get me closer to Mohammed. It was one of those nights where I simply couldn't stop thinking about him. His ocean blue eyes came like waves into my heart and I came to accept that I actually missed him so much. Without realizing what I was about to do, I picked up the phone and called him. I heard my heart beat get faster and faster as the phone started ringing.

"Miss me already?" said the heavenly voice on the other side of the phone. Yes, I do miss you. A lot.

"You randomly popped into my mind tonight, how's everything?" I asked trying to seem as normal as humanly possible.

"I'm doing good, I started university today… how about you? Any updates?"

"I'm going to complete high school and then hopefully, university. I already registered at a nearby school," I said, "I had a really bad day today," I added with hesitation. I don't know why I told him that but I really REALLY wanted to. I felt like there was someone poking at my heart urging me to tell him about my day even if it wasn't that eventful. I wondered if this was truly how it felt to love someone. Was this even love? I was unsure of everything but I was sure that I wanted him by my side. He let out a light laugh that made me subconsciously smile. "What's wrong?" I asked.

"Do you know that you space out a lot? I mean, I'm talking and suddenly the phone just goes silent," he lets out another chuckle, "anyways, what happened today?"

He was the first person to notice these small things about me and I notice small things about him as well like the way he mumbles when he reaches to the end of his sentence. I don't know why he did that, it seemed like something he naturally did; he mumbled a lot! And I know it sounds like an annoying thing to hear someone do but for some deranged reason, it was the cutest thing I had ever encountered. Oh god, I was spacing out again! "I'm sorry," I continued to talk about my day;

the Syrian girl I met, my thoughts about the world around me and finally concluding my day with my conversation with the counsellor. He seemed genuinely pleased to hear that I had a plan; I sometimes felt like God had sent him to me to try and fix all the things that were broken in me. To be completely honest, I had no idea what he was saying. My mind was focused on the feelings that I had started developing for this random guy that I met on an airplane. I laughed when he laughed and pretended like I was completely focused on what he was saying. I always considered myself as a good listener; I often engaged in deep conversations with Hanan in prison and I really put my focus on her solely but for some reason that I completely could not understand, I was unable to do the same with Mohammed. It was as if he had come from a completely different planet and we had a language barrier in front of us; I was more fascinated by his words than the conversation itself. It was as if although he spoke, it always sounded like he was reciting poetry and my ears were in absolute thirst to continue listening. Beauty was found in every word that came out of his mouth and I was truly mesmerized. Was it some sort of spell that was casted on me? I honestly didn't know but what I did know was that I didn't want to ever lose this feeling in my entire life. The conversation ended an hour into the phone call and as he closed the phone, I felt like the world's doors were closing down on me. The feeling of safety was no longer engulfing me and it was now, replaced with an intense sense of longing. It was just an unfamiliar urge to be beside someone I knew nothing about. When I stopped and actually thought about this relationship, or however I'd want to label it, I came to the realization that I'm completely hooked on someone who I don't know. I didn't know him. I didn't know how he was raised, what his morals are, what he stands for, how many siblings he had, if any. Nothing. So how could I feel so safe around someone who is nothing but a stranger? My mom always told me not to speak to strangers but this stranger has led me to a world that is bound to reach happiness. This was the first time I had deliberately not listened to one of my mom's advices and I didn't regret it; not even one bit. I tried to go to sleep but he was like a shot of strong coffee because my eyes were now wide open and there was nothing I could do about it. Sleep has now left my eyes and resided somewhere far away. For the first time in forever, I was left alone and instead of thinking about everything bad that was happening in the world; I started thinking about the good things. I was glad that I was alive and I was even more glad that I was alive with him.

An hour later and I had gone through many more failed attempts to fall asleep but it wasn't the kind of insomnia that made me feel miserable; it made me feel a kind of joy that I had never felt before. My eyes stayed wide open as I watched the sun rays start to slide through the edge of my curtain. My heart squeezed at the thought of spending another day without him by myside but I dismissed my thoughts straight away. The next few days were a blur of me studying and talking as much I possibly could with Mohammed. I never really understood the concept of labelling relationships whether they be romantic or friendly. I never understood the point of it… what difference does it make if we label ourselves or not? How we feel towards each other won't change in any way just because we have come to label what we have going on. I feel like labelling not only relationships but also people was a system used in the old ages to cause segregation between the people in the society and it has worked to this day. All these social constructs have led us to this point where we feel the need to label everything and this is what has caused us to feel uneasy towards those who think in a different manner than us, whether it be in a religious, political or social matter. The concept of having people with different views and ideologies is what actually has shaped our societies which is why I strongly believe that these differences should not be ignored or diminished but rather explored and accepted because without acceptance, we are never going to be able to benefit ourselves, first and foremost, and then our society.

One night, as Mohammed and I were talking, he suggested we meet. I was never a kind of person that got along with others on the phone. I had to see someone to feel connected to them. Isn't that how we all are? Online relationships are based solely on words and those words accumulate to nothing if we are physically unable to see facial expressions or actions. Spending time with someone is also what ties us to them, it gives us a sense of belonging and helps us find things we have in common and is basically a fuel to all our upcoming conversations. I never really had an online friend, I tried but I couldn't find the purpose of it. Some may argue that having online relationships can give you some sort of insight to the world outside but isn't that what we have the news for? I mean yes, news could be biased and words could be manipulated to support those biases but what we often forget is that people could also unintentionally be biased. That is something that I have recently found out; most people don't have pure intentions in their heart and seem to do things just for the sake of getting something out of it. I mean, why are governments so corrupt? Because yes, they do give us an access to education, roads or any form of a public good but in the same time, they're only doing that to gain power, support and money. Money. The most disgusting reward of them all; I know money is supposed to be something that we seek to have a comfortable life but it is a concept that has been the reason behind so many massacres. Can you believe that we kill each other for a piece of paper? I do understand that everything we do is to, in return, get something back but somethings are just ethically wrong.

But then again what are ethics? We can never come to a complete agreement when it comes to morals… when we really think about it, everything has a grey area. Now when you think about taking a life, your first thought would be that it's immoral but when you come to think more about it, what if that person is a serial killer and you know that keeping them around will only cause more deaths? Is killing them justified then? Or is taking a life never justified? There are many concepts that follow that same pattern of thinking; it's not hard to find a moral dilemma but rather to find something that everyone agrees to. I think at this point whoever you are, you can tell that I literally think about everything and anything. It's exhausting.

So back to my point, I agreed to meet Mohammed. One afternoon, I left to the park that's almost 10 minutes away from the shelter and I saw his soothing features from afar. He was sitting on the floor with his legs crossed; his eyes constantly moved as if he was looking for me, the moment his gaze locked mine, a warm smile appeared on his lips. I was suddenly filled with more unfamiliar feelings. I didn't know what I was feeling but I knew that I wanted to feel it for the rest of my life.

"I thought you weren't gonna come," he said. I was in fact half an hour later, I explained to him how I decided to walk from the shelter, thinking it was not that far. Walking alone in the streets is another new experience to me, as weird as it sounds. I never walked alone back in Palestine because my neighborhood wasn't safe. My mom always made sure there was someone with us whether it was her or any one of my siblings or family members. I felt completely at ease walking around two kilometers down a road I've never been to all myself. Walking alone made me collect my scattered thoughts in a way. I took a seat on the floor, right in front of him. He had arranged a picnic. How cliché. The grass below us was covered with a checkered red-blue carpet and there was a basket at the edge of the carpet. It was a simple arrangement but I could tell that he had put a lot of thought and effort into it. I appreciated what he did. I appreciated him. His sharp nose crinkled when he smiled and I was sure he had never noticed that but I did and it was beautiful. He told me about a Yemeni boy he met in university and how his story was similar to mine and although it all happened a long time ago, I felt a feeling of comfort knowing that there was a university student who went through the same things I went through and is fine. I wouldn't say he's in a good state of mind, no one ever is after they suffer from traumatic events but he was fine and that was good enough. This is the sad things about trauma, you never get over it, no matter how hard you try.

I spent three incredibly fast hours with the one person I felt at home with. It's weird how we associate home to the things that we love, don't you think? The concept behind that is that the people we love make us feel safe and so does our home but I never felt safe in my own home. My home was some sort of a constant battlefield. I was always frightened that I would wake up in the remains of a war and suddenly, one day, I did. My heart felt light as the thought of spending a lifetime with Mohammed floated into my mind; how childish of me! I felt like someone who had just gotten out of a battlefield and thrown into heaven; and that, was exactly how I'd explain my feelings towards moving here but in the same time, despite all of this, I knew I'd always love my battlefield of a country.

I read a lot of love stories but I never thought that it actually feels like this… I was told it's like a dream come true but before this, I didn't even dare to dream this far; to dream of a day where I felt safe. You know what I never really got though? Why couldn't we just live with the israelis? I knew it was a matter of power and not just religion… just like all the countries in the world, they were thirsty for power. The concept of power was the unclear part of all of this because I felt like power and politics didn't have the same goal. Politics was when advocates set policies or rules to be able to provide the public with services such as education, transportation or health care. Politics, in essence, is a very noble career path but sadly, has been manipulated by those who have different agendas to serve their own purposes. The most important thing in the world seems to be power and money; and there is nothing more toxic than that. I do understand that human beings are entitled to care for their own, in the end we are wild creatures and our main objective in the world is to survive. Our instinct tells us to survive despite who we throw under the bus. Now think of this logically, if you were driving and you knew that if you drive forward you'll be hit with a bus but if you stopped someone else would be hit by a bus, what would you do? Theoretically speaking, some would say they'd drive forward because they'd like to act noble and fearless but in the moment, no one will drive forward. Our instinct will make us subconsciously choose the safer side. A real life example of that would be that when you're driving and a car drives towards you, by instinct, you will swerve to the other lane; you're not going to stop and think that if you swerve you might crash into another car, you're just going to think that if you do it, there's a higher chance of you surviving. Actually, in fact... you're not even going to think. It's just going to happen... it's a natural instinct. So I understand why people have the thirst for power but what the israeli government is doing is utter nonsense, they are killing people in order to gain unnecessary power. There are many different things that you, as a person, can do to gain power but power like anything else, can be both a positive and a negative thing. With no doubt, the negative aspect to it is easier; the negative things are always easier to achieve. One of the principles I always follow in my life is to never seek something if the way to it could harm others or lower my own morals which is why I am never going to understand the concept of gaining power by hurting innocent people.

"I'm really glad I met you," I heard him suddenly say and my heart started fluttering in my chest.

"I'm glad I met you too," I replied.

We spent hours talking about our philosophies of life; he was one of those people that actually listened, I felt him drown in my words and I drowned in his. His voice was like a lullaby but it was a strange lullaby; it was a mixture of softness but also, anger. He always had some sort of anger in his voice and when I told him that, he said that I had the same anger in my eyes. I guess this is what happens when you're from an occupied country.

The sunlight faded and it was time to leave my comfort.

"When am I going to see you again?" he asked.

"When the sun rises again," I said and smiled softly.

"And when will it rise again?"

"When we're finally free."

I smiled one last smile and walk away. As I made further steps towards the end of the road, I kept on looking back to see him; he didn't leave. He just stood there and watched me walk back home. The further I walked, the heavier my heart felt. Was this all just because I was leaving him once again? I let the thoughts run freely around my head as I walked back to the shelter.

Chapter 9

"Where were you?" asked Fairooz with childish curiosity, it was as if she was the shelter's bodyguard since all she did was sit in the kitchen and see who enters or leaves the building.

"I was out," I smiled, "with a friend."

"A friend?" she smirked.

"Yeah, just a friend," I replied, uncertain of my own answer.

I spent the night studying with her, she tried her best to help me understand all the things I missed out on when I was in prison; the support she gave me was a kind of support no one has ever given me in my entire life. We spent the next week together studying and occasionally talking about Mohammed. I told her how we met and how I actually didn't know what we were but I knew that I felt safe with him by my side.

Fairooz told me about this new project that she was starting where she gave Palestinians who still live in Palestine the opportunity to contact her through email or phone and she would listen to their stories and try to help them in any way that she possibly could and of course, I decided to take part in her project. She helped me set up an email address and taught me how to use it. Being a humanitarian should be a human decency, it should be something that we all aspire to become however, it saddens me that people are turning more and more into selfish, power-thirsty individuals. We humans have ruined everything in the world. Medicine is supposed to be one of the most humanitarian careers in the world yet, people have been able to turn such a noble career into a business. I remember when I was a child, I fell and scraped my knee… it wasn't a big deal but I was bleeding so bad that it frightened my parents. I was rushed into the hospital by my father but the doctors refused to treat me merely because I couldn't afford the treatment. I thought doctors were supposed to help everyone regardless of who they are, what they do or what social class they belong to. The doctor left me to bleed and I was then treated by a family friend who went to multiple medical courses; she was not a doctor but she was good enough to help make the bleeding stop. My leg is still not a 100% okay to this day, if I run, I then have to limp for the rest of the day. The doctor's refusal to help me that day had an everlasting effect on my life. I am never going to forgive him. He was not even an israeli doctor; he was Palestinian just like me but you'd be surprised with what money can do. Money is such a dirty thing and the funny thing is that it's literally a piece of paper that was governmentally produced to be a means of trade and now, it's something that can decide to what extent people would trust you and how much you're really worth. It's a sick concept. Medicine is not the only noble career that has been dehumanized by us 'humans'. Law is also supposed to be a career where you defend the innocent but now, we just defend the person who can pay us well. The same goes to Politics and any other field you can possibly think of. The world is turning into a matter of money, power and monopoly and it's too frightening to even think about.

As I was about to leave to go to bed, I received a phone call. The number was unfamiliar but it was a Palestinian country code. My heart dropped. It was really late back in Palestine so this must have been an emergency. Holding on tight to my fragile heart, I picked up.

"Hello?"" I spoke as my voice shook with fear.

"I'm so sorry for calling you at this time," I heard the familiar sound of gunshots and bombs in the background and in a weird way, I felt nostalgic, "I don't know what else to do."

"Who is this?" I asked.

"I found your number in the Palestinian Crisis helpline. My house is being bombarded with bullets and tear gas."

"Are you okay?"

"I'm a bit wounded but I'll be fine," she took a pause and then breathed deeply, "my sister is not okay... I think she needs to be taken to a hospital."

"Are there any adults in the house?"

"My grandfather... he's handicapped though; he can't take me. I've called an ambulance but israeli forces have banned ambulances from entering my area."

"I will call for help and then get back to you," I softly said, "stay close to the phone."

"Are you going to leave me alone?" she said with her pleading voice. My heart ached as the pain she felt literally radiated into my chest. I wanted to tell her that everything will be okay but I was unsure.

"I'm not going anywhere. I'll call a medical emergency team and I will call you back."

"You promise?" she asked and I could now sense that she was younger than I thought.

"I promise," I replied softly and hung up the phone.

I actually didn't know what to do. I was not the kind of person who knew how to act during emergencies but the adrenaline was pumping through my veins and for the first time in a while, I felt alive and purposeful. I called the shelter back in Palestine and one of the volunteers picked the phone.

"Layal? Is everything okay?"

"I need your help," I hurriedly stated, "there's a girl who called... her house is being attacked and her sister is heavily wounded. Ambulances have been cut off, there's no one in her house who can drive and she needs immediate medical care."

"Do you know what kind of wound it is?"

"No, I don't but it sounded really serious. She was attacked with guns and tear gas. Please get someone."

"We'll send our medical team right now, please text me her address."

I hung up the phone and quickly sent them the address and then called the girl again. She picked up on the first ring.

"I thought you wouldn't call back."

"I'm back and I arranged for me a medical team to come to your location. Can your sister speak?"

"I tried talking to her but she wouldn't reply," she answered helplessly. I could feel her frustration. It's weird how much you can understand a person's personality when you see how they act in stressful situations. I could tell that although this girl sounded young, she was the one who took the responsibility to take care of her family. She was probably the eldest sister. I sympathized with her because I remember how it felt when I lost my sister. I wasn't sure if her sister was even alive but I knew that she was in a lot of pain. The worst part was that I was too far to physically be there for her and there was nothing that made me more upset. I wished if I was there with her.

"What's your name?" I asked her.

"Noor," she replied.

"Can you do something for me?" I didn't wait for her answer and continued talking, "hold your sister's arm and feel the vein that is on her arm, diagonally under her thumb."

"Okay."

"Do you feel something?"

"Yes," she said, I could feel a sense of hopefulness and happiness start to make its way to her heart.

"That's good, how old is your sister?"

"Four."

"Okay, can you turn her to her right side… make sure one of her arms is placed under head."

I could hear her movements through the phone as she tried to move her sister and then I heard the phone fumble.

"Are you there?" I asked but couldn't get a reply. I could hear a lot of noise but I couldn't understand what was being said.

"We're here," I recognized the voice. The volunteers had made it to her house. I felt an unbelievable sense of relief.

"What's the situation?" I asked. I was in the safe side of the world and I felt furious for being here. I really wished I could be of direct help.

"The sister is stable, she has a bullet in her leg though and has fainted due to great loss of blood but it's going to be fine. The team took her to one of our doctors back at the shelter. They'll take care of her."

"What about the girl I was talking to?"

"The grandfather passed away of trauma… we're taking her to the shelter with us. Her sister too, after she's well enough," she said, "she keeps on asking to see you though."

"Hand her the phone."

I heard the sound of the phone being shuffled around.

"You're not here?" she asked, the amount of sadness in her voice accumulated onto my chest once again.

"No, I'm in another country… Norway, have you heard of it?"

"No," she replied innocently.

"Are you okay?" I asked.

"I'm scared."

I felt a strong urge pulsate down my spine; I wanted to be back in my country. I know it's a noble thing to work towards change wherever you are in the world but I wanted to be in Palestine. I wanted to be a part of the field work there. It was such a stupid thing for me to attempt to make a change in Palestine while I'm living a happy and comfortable life thousands of miles away. Anger radiated through me. Why did I ever decide to leave? How selfish could I possibly be to leave my own country and live in a world of comfort? Yes, there were a lot of people who moved here and settled but my body itched with the idea of making a difference and I knew I couldn't make it here. I always felt like one of the special ones. God threw all kinds of tests at me but I always managed to get over them sooner or later and these tests were not just God's way of making me suffer. No! They were his way of giving me strength and making sure that I have what it takes to use my experiences to help others, or that's how it felt at the very least.

"The place they're taking you… I lived there," I said slowly, trying my best to comfort her, "you'll meet people and you'll make friends, I'm still friends with one of the girls I met there a long time ago. The volunteers are also great support systems; I know it's hard to get yourself to start talking to them but once you do, I promise you'll feel better."

"You promise?" she pleaded once again.

"I promise."

She hung the phone up and I could only imagine that she had taken my advice. Worry fluttered its way into my chest and I couldn't help but think of her all night long. Was she okay? Was she going to wake up with a gun pointing at her face like I did? I really hope she doesn't go through what I went through. I felt uneasy the entire night and couldn't sleep because of how much I was filled with worry.

My morning alarm rang and I immediately turned it off. I was contemplating a decision in my head; should I stay here and complete my education or go back to Palestine and be a social worker? Of course, my phone rang at the perfect time and it was Mohammed.

"You okay?" he asked as soon as I picked up.

"I really don't know… I've got a lot on my mind."

"What's on your mind?"

"I'm thinking of going back to Palestine," I talked as quickly as I could because I knew he wouldn't accept my plan, "I want to be a social worker there. I know it's risky but I really want to do it. This is a cause I'm willing to sacrifice myself for."

"What about your education?" he sensibly asked.

"I have the basic skills and I can do school online. I'll sort it out with the shelter and refugee school."

"Don't be impulsive, Layal," he sharply said.

"I'm not being impulsive. I don't think I can live with myself knowing that there are people struggling back there."

"You can't save the world."

"I can try!", he was now getting on my nerves. I knew that what I wanted to do would not going to easily be accepted by him and I didn't expect him to clap for me but I also didn't expect him to directly stand in my way and try to bring me down.

"I'm leaving," I said, already making my decision, "I love you but I can't stay here with my hands crossed and watch the world around me tear to shreds. There are people who need me."

"If you feel like it's the right decision then do it but I can't support you. You're of no use when you're dead."

He hung up the phone without giving me a chance to reply. I couldn't understand why he was acting that way but I knew that no matter what he says, I needed to do what my heart was telling me to do or else I will always live in a sort of grief over what I could have done but didn't. It absolutely saddened me that I didn't get his support but I could just hope that eventually, he will be able to think of it the way I had and come to terms with it. I made my way to the kitchen where Fairooz and her friends were having breakfast. I realized that I actually hadn't talked to anyone except Fairooz and the volunteers since I've been here. "Good morning," said Fairooz with her usual jolly vibe.

"Good morning," I said, "have you seen the educational advisor?"

"She's in the common area."

I immediately made my way there. I knew it would take some convincing for her to allow me to get home schooled but I had a good argument in my defense.

I felt my heart drop as I made my way to the common area. I knew that in the end, whatever I wanted would happen. Despite the fact that I really tried to attempt to hide how I felt, I was unsure of everything after my conversation with Mohammed. I felt as though he was somewhere above holding me back no matter how hard I tried to move. I knew that my vision was too idealistic but I also knew that staying in Europe was completely useless. The volunteer looked at me as soon as I walked into the common area. It was almost as if she was waiting for me.

"Is everything okay?" she immediately asked. My anxiety was visible from the way I looked. My face had turned pale because I had lost my ability to sustain basic life after that phone call. I could tell she was genuinely interested in what I was saying because her iris grew wider as she waited for me to speak.

"Did you change your mind?" she asked, trying to give me a foundation to speak on. I don't know why but I suddenly lost my ability to speak. You know when you've got something so heavy on your chest but you're physically unable to let it out? That was exactly how I felt.

"Can I get homeschooled?" I asked her, afraid to hear the answer that I was going to get.

"Why?"

"I want to work in field work… I can't stay here and live comfortably whilst there are many people out there who are suffering. I just can't. I'm sorry," my voice started quivering, "I know I said I want to continue my education and I do want to do that but I'm not sure if I can. I literally won't be able to focus on my work because my mind is all the way back in Palestine."

"If I give you the green light to go back there, what are you planning to do? I mean, I know you want to make a change but have you got any ideas as to how you're going to do it?"

"I know it's not as ideal as it sounds but I want to start working with the shelter there. I want to be part of the voluntary work. Like yesterday, a girl called me and she needed help. The feeling I felt realizing that I couldn't physically be there for her and help her directly was unbearable and I know many more phone calls are going to come my way and I need to actually be there to help."

"Is this about what happened last night?" she asked, trying to understand my point of view. This is what I loved about the volunteers, they had a very open mind. Although I knew for a fact that she didn't agree with what I was saying, she still tried to get my point.

"You can't let one event effect you this much. What will you do when you witness a death of someone you've grown attached to?"

"I don't know… but I do know that I want to be there no matter what."

"Look, the only reason I'm not supporting this is because you're letting one event determine your whole life course," she said and then continued, "you need to think of this decision in the long term, will you be able to cope? I get that it's something you want to do and trust me when I tell you that each and every Palestinian here wants to do the same thing but we need to look at it more logically. Not only is this whole thing too idealistic but it's also very risky; I can't even guarantee that you'll even make it to the shelter alive."

"I'm willing to take the risk," I may have been impulsively speaking but my heart burned with passion. We all have reasons to live and I guess this one's mine. There are things that are worth dying for and I'm willing to sacrifice my life to this cause.

"Sleep on it."

I had made my decision but she had convinced me to wait a bit longer. I wanted to say that nothing will happen in a couple of days but I knew, in my country, a lot could happen in even a couple of minutes. I decided to let this go to rest for a while. I left the common area in frustration and went back to my room. A few minutes later, I heard a knock at the door and it was Fairooz. I was supposed to be studying with her for the school's admission test but I skipped today's lesson so it was no surprise that she came to see me. Before she could even ask me what was wrong, I told her everything. I told her about last night's phone call and how it had changed my perspective about my future. It had given me a vision that I wasn't sure I could bring to life but I was certain that I wanted to pursue. She gave me the reaction that everyone else did; that I shouldn't do it. I didn't expect that kind of reaction from her because she to, was a revolutionary. The hotline service idea was hers so technically, she ignited this fire in me. She said that what I wanted to do was illogical, that I would be useless without an education, that I would be useless if I was killed or arrested again and the list continued. People kept reciting the disadvantages of moving back to Palestine, they never really understood that I was completely aware and there is nothing worse than wanting to do something so bad but not finding anyone who's willing to support you. In a way, it just felt like people were telling me that want I wanted to accomplish wasn't accomplishable…. I knew that they didn't want it to come out this way to me but I felt like no one believed in me. It was a completely illogical thought and I knew that but how could you make someone format something from their brain when they have continuously been hearing it? I was told that no matter what decision I were to make, I'd always be supported but in reality, I wasn't.

Fairooz could now sense the mental turmoil I was going through and tried to do the impossible to make feel a little more at ease but that wasn't possible anymore. My heart was telling me to just drop everything and leave but how could I leave when I couldn't even afford a plane ticket. Matter of fact, I couldn't even afford a bottle of water without the help of the shelter. What if I get a part time job? Will it really be that hard knowing that I don't have any sort of education? I knew I wanted to pursue a career in social work but I didn't know where and how to start. My thoughts spiraled alongside my sanity. I wanted to leave. The reality was that although I knew I was safe, nothing felt like home anymore. I was in a world where nothing felt familiar. The unfamiliarity was slowly driving me to a part of myself that I never knew existed; a part where everything was dark and there was nothing I could do about it but leave. My warzone of a country felt like a better alternative as to this place that could easily be a replica of what heaven could be like. I wasn't sure if I'd ever make it heaven but I prayed that my parents were there. Is it weird that I would rather live in a battle zone than somewhere far away from my country?

"Personally, I don't support your decision to leave but I know you well enough to know that you you're going to leave regardless of what I think," she cut off my train of thought, "so if you must leave then leave but at least have a sensible plan… don't be impulsive because you'll then do nothing but harm yourself."

She really had a point, and so I continued to think about my decision. Should I do it? Should I not do it? I honestly couldn't come to a final decision since my thoughts were all over the place. I was never the kind of person who often engaged in physical activity but without a second thought, I found myself going for a run and let me tell you this: you'd be surprised of the effect a run has on your disturbed thoughts. It has a steady twenty minutes run and I found myself back in my room. I never competed or took part in sports but I had a good physical capacity because of how much I had to run –for my life, in Palestine. For a reason that I could not even fathom, I decided to call Mohammed.

"What?" he immediately asked, I could sense the anger in his tone… he was fed up.

"I'm sorry, I know you're upset… but this is a personal decision and I never meant to hurt you with it but it's just something that I have to do… it doesn't feel right to sit here with my hands crossed."

"I just don't see the point of risking the whole life you've created here for something that could possibly not even happen," he said in a matter of fact way and gave a sigh that came from the depths of his heart. For a second, I contemplated letting all of this go, to ease his pain a bit.

"I'm not putting my life on the line, Mohammed. I'm fighting for a cause that I believe in, a cause that you should believe in too and I don't think there's anything that I could do in my life that would make me as proud and as happy as I'd be when I'm fighting for my country."

"You're not fighting for your country, you're killing yourself. You're literally just walking into death or prison."

"I would rather die or rot in prison than stay here, not doing anything."

"I don't even know why I'm arguing with you about this. You and I both know that when you decide something, nothing I or anyone else says will be able to change your mind. You have already made your mind and programmed your brain to stop accepting any comment that is not in support of your decision," he took a deep breath again, "so go ahead, do as your heart desires."

He hung up the phone before I could even reply to what he said. Feelings of guilt starting roaming around my mind. I loved Mohammed and I didn't want to upset him but I knew that I loved my country more and God wouldn't have put such an urge in me if it didn't accumulate to anything in the end. Yes, I was going to do what my heart desired, even if he disagreed. In the end, there are millions of Mohammeds and just one Palestine. And I, was willing to sacrifice everything for my Palestine even if it meant losing the ones that I love. It almost felt like I was constantly losing people and things for the sake of Palestine (my family, my friends, my house and my loved ones) but it was alright, everything could be replaced or at least, I could move on from all those things but I could never move on from the place I was born in, the place I had my first steps in and the place I lost to those Zionists. Feelings of pride started to overcome the guilt that I was previously feeling. I was and will always be a proud Palestinian and my country comes above every other thing in my life; there was no person, thing or place that could possibly take the enormous place Palestine has in my heart.

Although I tried to tell myself that I was certain of what I wanted to do, I wasn't. This strong feeling I felt mixed with the inexplicable feelings of uncertainty were starting to eat at my heart. What was worse than this feeling was the fact that I actually had no one to talk to anymore. In a way, I felt like I lost everyone. I didn't have the audacity to even call Mohammed after telling him that I was going to leave regardless of how he felt about it and I couldn't talk to Fairooz because she thought my idea of leaving was ridiculous and would bring me down every time I talked about it. I took long runs to the park where I saw Mohammed in, in hopes of 'accidentally' seeing him but I never did. I missed my school interview and my mental state spiraled from a state of euphoria to a state of utter misery. The only safe haven I knew was my bed; it was my comfort every time I felt like I could no longer live. I came to accept that I was never going to see Mohammed again and that I had done too much damage to fix it and plus… despite all these feelings, I always had one goal which was to return to Palestine so if we didn't have the same goal, this would've happened sooner or later.

Chapter 10

After days filled with lack of sleep, lack of food and lack of water, I had reached a level of exhaustion that I couldn't even physically leave my bed. I heard a knock at my door, it didn't sound like Fairooz, Fairooz basically broke my door every time she knocked it.

"Yes," my voice was hardly audible, "who is it?"

The door was pushed open and as soon as I saw the career advisor, I gave out a big sigh. I wasn't in the mood to listen to her ramble on and on about my options. I knew my options! I have memorized my options! I need a way out, not just someone reciting options, pros and cons to me.

"You still hate me?" she asked jokingly.

"I don't hate you," I let out a small laugh. I don't hate her, I'm sick of listening to her while she spoke about things I've heard a thousand times before.

"I don't know about that but you definitely won't after you see what I have for you," she reached into her bag and gave me a piece of paper; it was an airplane ticket, "I know you're still uncertain but I think you should go. I've had people who come here and insist on leaving a few days later but when we shut them down, they quickly get over it. I think you're meant to be there and not here."

I examined my ticket to make sure this isn't a joke, "and my education?" I asked in concern.

"Don't worry about your education. I will set up a home schooling program and send it to you on your email and I know focusing on field work and school in the same is going to be a challenge but I know that if you want it, you'll make it. So go on, don't make me regret this decision."

"Are you serious?" my eyes popped wide open; I couldn't come to understand that she had allowed me to leave this easily.

"I'm serious," she calmly said and gave me a warm smile, "I talked to the shelter back in Palestine and they told me all about how you were able to save a young girl's life while being thousands of miles away. Do you know it was your first aid instructions that were able to save that child's life? You have a lot of potential but please, please, don't be impulsive. It's a dangerous place and working there is going to get you in trouble so please think before you do anything, your death or arrest is not going to benefit anyone. Keep that in your mind."

"I will. I promise." I quickly said, she gave me some documents.

"I'll take you to the airport tomorrow morning. Be ready."

"Thank you." I watched her as she left the room. I felt as though I was in a virtual world where everything I ever wanted came to life. I couldn't believe that they let me leave. I often said that I would leave by myself but to be completely honest, in addition to the fact that I had absolutely no money, I also had no idea how to book a ticket. I was shocked to know that airports had distinctive names. I thought the airport of Norway was literally just called "Norway Airport" but it's not; it has some distinctive name I've never heard of. There were a lot of things that normal people would know at young ages that I still didn't know because of my closed life. My parents always kept me closed off to protect me from things that happened from the other side of our house's door. My parents were very peaceful people, they often got bashed for it. They never took part in politics and demonstrations because they believed that no matter what we do, nothing will change as soon as israel is being backed up by the major countries in the world such as the US. What affected us the most was that although the US supported israel, it still gave funds to Palestinian refugees. Those funds that were worth millions of dollars and helped millions of refugees were cut off by the current US president, Donald Trump. Trump doesn't seem to realize how his decisions affect the lives of millions of people; I honestly don't know if he's too dumb to understand what responsibilities his position entitles him to have. First he declares Jerusalem as the capital of Israel and then he cuts off our funds? Who does he think he is? I'm pretty sure his whole presidency was just a big scam. How could such an idiot be given so much power? This is why I'm so skeptical about the idea of power. I couldn't come to understand how someone so dumb could end up being the president of a major country in the world. What I have to admit though is that he is not as dumb as we think, he's a genius but his priorities are messed up. The whole trump presidency is live evidence to the selfishness that is within us. He won the elections by votes and so you'd think if he was so stupid why would he be voted for? Well, he vocalized his racist and selfish thoughts as to how we could "make America great again" and sadly, the idea of making America the capital of the world, even if it includes hurting others to get this amount of power, was attractive to many American citizens.

There was a certain urge that I felt deep within my heart; it was an unavoidable urge to call Mohammed. I had to at least tell him I was leaving tomorrow. While getting ready for a negative reaction, I slowly picked the phone up and dialed his number. He picked up but refused to speak first.

"I'm sorry," I broke the silence, "I know you're hurt but I have to do this… I really do Mohammed and if you can't bring yourself to understand and accept my point of view then I guess great things require us to endure great amounts of pain and leaving you is the pain I must endure."

"When are you leaving?" his voice broke as he spoke.

"Tomorrow morning."

"I want to see you. Twenty minutes? At the park?"

"I'll see you there," I said and hung up the phone. I was so anxious to see him; I didn't know if I even had the audacity to face him. After the way that I was just going to leave him? How could I? I was curious as to what he was going to tell me, I hoped that he had found it in his heart to forgive him. I really prayed that he would move back to Palestine with me but I knew that was a stretch and it was a selfish thing for me to want of him. In the end, it was his life and he had to do what his heart desires just like how I was going to do what mine desired. I knew that if I was in his position, I would probably have reacted in the exact same way that he did, probably even worse, so I really respected him for still wanting to talk to me after my betrayal. Was it a betrayal if I was leaving for a noble cause? I don't know. I had planned to walk to the park but quickly found myself running to it… I was so eager to see him and listen to what he had to say. This was either going to be our grand finale or just our beginning. I pray for the latter. He was already at the park when I made it there, I saw his dark hair from afar and although I was very eager to see him, I was also very nervous. I found my footsteps getting heavier and slower every time I took a closer step to him. It felt like I took forever to make my way to where he was sitting.

"Hey," I said, "I'm really glad to see you."

"Are you really…" he took a pause and I could see the sadness in his ocean eyes, "leaving?"

I immediately looked down at the ground beneath me, hating that I have caused someone who could possibly be the love of my life all this pain. "I'm sorry."

"Don't be… this is something that you really want to day," he sighed and it felt like his words were heavy on his tongue, "yes, I do think its dumb but I can't withhold you from doing something that you really want to do." His hands slowly made their way to me and he cupped my hands in his; his hands were as soft as his heart. I couldn't believe that he was starting to accept that I was leaving and wasn't very angry about it. His fingers started playing with mine until he suddenly looked up and said, "I'm going to miss you."

My heart felt warmer and his words were now like symphonies in my ears. They eased me the way sad music eases someone who's depressed.

"I'm going to miss you too."

"In these few weeks, you have given me more than anyone ever has in a lifetime. I'm so glad I got to know you and I just wanted to let you know that I love you more than you'll ever know. No matter what happens, you'll always have me with you right in your heart."

I was now embarrassed of how I could leave someone who means so much to me so easily. Or he might think I'm leaving this easily but it's not as easy as he thinks. I know this is going to be the hardest decision that I'll ever make but I've learned that there are some things that we just have to do and this was one of them.

"Good bye," I said, "until we meet again."

"And when will we meet again?"

"Whenever the sun rises again," I softly said.

"And when will the sun rise again?" he asked.

"When we're finally free," I replied.

I hugged him and felt my heart leave my body and enter his and I knew that it was time to officially say goodbye. I could feel my tears slowly make their way down my cheek and I saw the tears make their way down his. He wiped my tears with his hand and kissed my forehead. It was time to leave. And so, I left.

Chapter 11

I walked back to the shelter with my mind preoccupied with thoughts of him. I didn't know how I felt about meeting him. On one hand, I felt very relieved knowing that he has forgiven me for leaving but on the other hand, my love for him grew in an unexpected way. I now felt like I wanted to spend the rest of my life with him although I knew I no longer could. There is something about wanting a person more when you can't have them and that was exactly what was happening to me. Sadly, just like he came to terms with the fact that I was leaving, I also had to come to terms with the fact that whatever we had was over. I loved him but I had to move on. There were things in my life that were much greater than a relationship. My thoughts were abruptly interrupted with a knock that was heard through the door as the counsellor walked into my room.

"Are you ready for tomorrow?" she asked enthusiastically as if I was going on a field trip.

"As ready as I can possibly be," I replied faintly.

"Did anything happen? Do you need to talk about it?"

I looked at my hands and felt her slowly make her way to my desk chair. She had a seat and looked at me, patiently waiting for me to speak.

"I feel guilty for leaving the people that I love behind."

"Fairooz? Oh she'll be fine!"

"No, not Fairooz. I know she'll be fine but I met a guy on my way here and we started seeing each other and now, I'm simply just going to leave him."

"How much does this guy mean to you?"

"A lot more than I initially thought. I saw him today… I said goodbye. He said he didn't understand why I want to leave but I should do as my heart desires. My heart is torn between leaving and staying."

"Emotions fade Layal. Never base your judgement based on how you feel about someone, especially at this age, I am not completely happy about your plan of going back to Palestine but I wouldn't want you to say here if it was simply for a guy. A year from now you might not even talk to him anymore so would you literally base your life decision on him?"

"I guess not," I replied and I knew that I appeared calm but my insides were turning into tsunamis and hurricanes…. I knew I shouldn't let my life revolve around him but because of the love I had for him; I was unsure of everything.

"How long have you known this guy for?"

"I literally met him on my way here. He was sitting next to me in the airplane and he talked very philosophically to me and something just clicked. We clicked."

She took a deep breath, "I think its best if you leave. If you had any other reason for wanting to stay, then I would have most definitely encouraged you to do so but your reason is an emotional one and there is no guarantee that he's going to be here forever. What happens when he leaves?"

"What happens when he doesn't?"

"You're seventeen, you've got a lot ahead of you… you're going to meet people and go places; it's too early to base your life around a guy. You're going to have a lot of time to do that once you get married."

Her remark about marriage hit a nerve in me and my train of thoughts started again. Was marriage really what she claimed it to be? If married was all about basing everything around a man, then why do people even get married? I never understood how marriage was constantly bashed yet everyone was so eager to get married. The hypocrisy! I remained quiet as I let those thoughts wonder in my head.

"So, I'll see you tomorrow morning?" she broke the silence.

"Yes, I'll be ready."

"Did you finish packing already?"

"Yes," I didn't have much to pack, just a couple of shirts and two pants, that was literally it. She grabbed my suitcase and informed me that it will be put in the reception area of the shelter to be taken to the car early morning before our car ride to the airport. Tomorrow was going to be an interesting day. Before going to bed, I prayed that God will lead me to wherever was best for me and make everything easier. And of course, I prayed to God to keep Mohammed safe.

I woke up to a missed call from Mohammed and so, I immediately called him back.

"Good morning," he said as soon as he picked up.

"Good morning," I replied.

"I just called to tell you to take care of yourself," his voice cracked as he continued, "have a safe flight and try to stay as safe as you can there. I love you."

"I love you."

"What time are you leaving?"

"I'm leaving in an hour… I'm just finalizing everything and I need to confirm with the shelter."

"Have a safe flight."

"Thank you," I replied and we stayed in a comfortable silence. I stayed quiet and listened to him breathe. Nothing could have possibly been more soothing. I felt at ease and I prayed that this wouldn't be our last conversation.

"Sadly, I have to go get ready," I broke the silence.

"Until we meet again," he said.

"Until we meet again," I replied and then hung up the phone. Oh God! I really was leaving!

I stopped myself from overthinking and driving myself crazy and got up to get ready. I left my room and knocked on Fairooz's door, was it weird that this was the first time I had gone to her room?

"Yes?" I heard from the other side of the door, "who's this?"

I opened the door and she immediately hugged me.

"You're really leaving?" she sadly spoke.

"I'm going to miss you a lot."

"I'm going to miss you a lot more. Stay in touch."

"I promise to stay in touch as long as I have a connection… you

know how it is there."

"I know… and if you come across any of the girls in the shelter, tell them I say hi and I miss them a lot. I think some of them should still be staying there," she took a very long pause and then spoke from the depth of her heart, "I'm so proud of you."

I felt my heartbeat slow-down in ease and a smile automatically formed on my face. This was the first time anyone has ever told me that they're proud of me and coming from Fairooz meant so much. I had always looked up to Fairooz, she had the strongest personality I have ever come across. I aspired to be just like her; someone who wanted to make a change. They always say that it's the crazy ones that believe they can change the world and to that I reply, Fairooz and I are the craziest people in the universe. I didn't know what to reply, she had put a sense of happiness in my heart that I was never going to get over.

"You don't need to say anything," she spoke as if she could read my mind, "just know that I'm extremely proud of the person you have become and I hope you end up fulfilling your goal. I know it's a very hard thing to accomplish but I also do know that you're one of the people who really work for what they believe in. Good luck."

"Thank you," I replied quickly and was just as quickly out of words, "I promise to do the best that I can do."

"I know you will," she smiled and gave me a hug, "have a safe flight."

I said my goodbyes and went back to my room to grab my last minute travel necessities and was soon accompanied by the counselor who said that it was time to leave. I followed her to the car and texted Mohammed as soon as I had a seat.

"I'm leaving now. I'm going to miss you." I pressed send.

"How do you feel about all of this today?" the career counsellor tried to initiate a conversation as soon as she started driving.

"I'm certain I want to do this," I replied, "I mean, yes, I am upset that I'm leaving everyone behind but I think I'd be more upset sitting here waiting for someone to be bold enough to help my own people. They're my people… it's my responsibility."

"Personally, I don't think you're responsible…. It's the major powers of the world that are responsible and the united nations of course. You're taking responsibility for something that you're not responsible for."

"Major countries and the UN are responsible of freeing my country, which they are obviously not doing a great job at, I'm responsible of helping my people personally. If your family members were in a dangerous position, wouldn't you do anything to help them? and if you can't help them, wouldn't you at least try everything that is within your power? Of course you will and you won't rest until you do so. My people are the closest thing I have to a family and I am willing to sacrifice everything, including myself, for their sake."

That reply was enough to keep her quiet for a while and I was happy to have a bit of silence. I knew that she didn't say anything wrong but what she said made me start to second guess myself and I really didn't want to do so. People have told me that the minute I start second guessing; it shows that I'm unsure of everything but I believe that second guessing is part of our nature. No matter how sure I was of something if someone were to talk negatively about it in front of me, I would start to rethink everything.

She kept quiet until we made it to the airport. She walked with me as I got my bags and checked me in.

"Good luck," she said, "have a safe flight."

"Thank you for everything," I replied.

Fear made its way out of my eyes and down my cheeks in the form of tears. She immediately hugged me and told that it was going to be alright.

"And you'll always have a home here," she said, "no matter what happens."

I felt so safe in Norway and the sad thing was I knew that this feeling of safety will diminish as soon as I get on that airplane but I had to do what I had to do. I said my goodbyes and walked into the departure area of the airport. People rushed in and out from all sides and I felt dizzy and lost in the crowd of people around me. I was going to miss this busy and lively atmosphere. Palestine is not like that. You smell heartache there. When you walk into a country where everything is broken, you don't see people rushing because they're busy, you see them rushing to find a place of safety. I couldn't wait to smell the scent of my country. I missed everything there was to miss from the sad atmosphere to the tea to the bread and cheese to the heartbreak. I missed everything. I was so glad to finally go home and I couldn't imagine my life to be any better. Oh, wait… The only thing that would be better was if Mohammed would come home with me, but I knew that was an impossible thing to ask.

As boarding started, I made my way into the airplane and had a seat. I was struck with a sense of disappointment when I didn't see Mohammed on the seat next to me. I rested my hand on the window by my seat and rested my head on it. I tried to slumber into a deep sleep and I did… I only woke up when the plane was already flying. I moved to another country to try and find a sense of safety and peace but I went back home just as quick as I left it. Was it even possible to find a place to call home other than your own country? I really didn't think so. The airplane was entirely filled with israelis; all I heard was Hebrew. A feeling of sadness overcame me. My country was populated with strangers and they have ruined all my beautiful memories. I remembered my family and prayed to God to have mercy on them and place them in the highest levels of heaven… I prayed that he accepts all the martyrs we have sacrificed for him.

It was easy to sleep in airplane as Mohammed wasn't there… he talked a lot on the plane ride here, he kept me up all night. I went into a deep sleep for the rest of the plane ride and only woke up on two occasions: when food was distributed and when we had finally arrived.

As soon as the airplane landed, I felt a sense of joy overcome me. I felt at home. Finally. I caught myself smiling as soon as I looked out the window and saw the most familiar and loving place in the universe, my Palestine.

I felt as light as a feather as I made my way out of the airplane and into the airport. For the first time, I actually had baggage to collect. The shelter in Norway provided me with a couple of t-shirt and pants so I could keep myself decent. The clothes weren't of best materials but they did just fine. I wasn't the kind of person who gave too much attention to materialistic things, mostly because I never had the opportunity to do so, but also I feel much more free because of it. As long as I'm wearing something, why should I be so concerned as to how pricey it is? Out of poverty, I was often forced to wear the same shirt for months or even years so knowing that I can change every other day was good enough for me. Someone once told me that the more money you have, the more money you subconsciously waste. As in if your salary is 2000 dollars, your necessities will equal 1500 whilst if your salary was 200, your necessities would probably equal around 100 and honestly, it is accurate. Humans are by nature selfish and greedy, nothing is enough for them which is why no matter what we do or how much money and power we have, we always strive for more. Of course that's a positive thing as you strive to be better but it could also be negative. An example of this could be the fact that 70% of our earth is made up of water which means that we have more water than we could possibly need. Nonetheless, that does not stop us from seeking to find water on other planets. Now why would we want water from another planet if we have more than enough on Earth? Greed. Yes, that's the answer. The problem isn't that we're just looking for resources, no, we tend to destroy the Earth we have right here to look for something that we don't really need. In the past couple of years, pollution has reached an extreme level as we are industrializing, more fossil fuels are burned which means more pollution and all of this for what? We have everything that we could possibly need. There are drawbacks to this phenomenon yet it can still be seen in a positive way; there are many ways that would make this phenomenon positive however, sadly; we have chosen to only water the aspects that are negative… that are ruining our Earth. And after destroying our planet, we even dare to call ourselves smart. We are embedded with so much greed for money and power that we don't even realize that we're destroying ourselves and everything that we have.

One of the volunteers from the shelter was at the airport waiting for me; she was the same volunteer who gave me a ride from my house to the shelter years ago. Nostalgia made its way to my heart. I didn't even know it was possible to feel nostalgic to something that caused you pain but I guess this is what happens when the only thing you have to look back on is pain. Pain and Loss. That was it.

"I'm so happy to see you as a strong grown woman… this is what we as volunteers live for, the sense of pride when we see people like you turn into these amazing human beings," she said.

"I wouldn't have been here if it wasn't for your help," I replied.

"It is your own effort that has made you reach this level of independence and intellectuality," she spoke as we walked in the parking lot and had a seat in the car, "are you ready to be a part of us?"

"Yes," I replied, "is the girl from the other day still in the shelter?"

"Yes she is and I'm sure that she'll be glad to see you. She was asking about you for a while."

"I'd be happy to see her as well… she was my push to come back and work here… I know I always idealistically wanted to be here but I didn't expect to actually do it, not this soon."

"A very few amount of people actually come back… I mean everyone leaves with the idea of returning but once they settle, they just realize it's easier to build a life there than here and it is, to be completely honest. Still, I feel like I won't feel true joy unless I'm truly making a difference and I can't do that back there."

"When I decided that I want to come back here, literally everyone told me it's a bad decision to the point where I started questioning myself and my goals… it took a lot of thinking but I realized that I'd rather be miserable here than comfortable there."

The volunteer was very supportive as she should be since I literally followed her path but the support I received made me feel at ease and finally confident with my decision to come back here. At Norway, a lot of people made me feel like what I had decided was the worst decision to ever be taken in history and although I pretended like it didn't have an effect on me, it really did. So finally listening to someone who understood what I exactly meant and supported me to be the person I feel I was destined to be, made me feel at ease.

Chapter 12

Joy electrified my nerves as I saw the shelter that I once considered my home. As soon as we reached, I immediately jumped out of the car and made my way into the shelter. This is what home feels like. As I walked into the shelter, a little girl came running to me.

"They told me you'd come! I couldn't wait any longer… I've been waiting all day. Do you remember me? You saved my sister's life," she spoke so quickly out of excitement.

Yes, I did remember her. She was the little girl who was literally my push to move all the way back here. She looked even younger than what she sounded like on the phone and so my heart shred into pieces when I saw her innocent young face and realized what she had to go through.

"I'm so glad to finally meet you," I said as I leaned down to hug her, "where's your sister?"

"She's right there," she pointed at a room on the other side of the corridor.

"Is she alright?" I asked.

"Yeah, so much better."

The little girl skipped back to her room and I took my luggage to the room I was assigned to. I always thought the volunteers had better rooms than us but no, the rooms were exactly the same. I looked out the window to see the broken down buildings that have been bombed around us and I reminisced on the days where I looked out my window in Norway and looked at the beautiful view of green fields and rivers.

"Are you all settled in?" asked the volunteer as she peeked into my room.

"Yes."

"Alright then let's get to work."

"Already?"

"Yeah, already! We've got a lot of things to do!"

"Alright then."

"Meet us in the meeting room upstairs in ten minutes."

And it just hit me that I was no longer the one being taken care of but rather the one taking care of others and there was absolutely nothing more frightening than that. I gathered all the things that I needed and made my way to the meeting room upstairs. I had never been in this room before. I saw around 15 volunteers gathered up in the hall. Their faces jerked up as soon as they heard me step into the room.

"Welcome home," said the leader volunteer.

"Thank you."

"Is everyone here?" she asked again and then took a quick attendance sheet and called out the names, making sure that everyone was here for the meeting.

"As you all know, we have a new volunteer working for us, her name is Layal," she took a pause and then continued, "let's give her a big round of applause for taking such a brave decision to come back and work here at this young age."

They all clapped and I felt embarrassed. I never wanted to do this to get recognition or credit... I believe that helping others is my duty as a human being and not something that I was supposed to be given a round of applause for. I looked at the floor until they finished clapping for me.

"Anyways, we have a big project coming up... Tomorrow, electricity and water will be shut off to the people on the eastern side of the area. We will be moving them here for a couple of hours and providing them with everything that they need until the israeli occupation opens up all sources of electricity and water tomorrow."

"Layal, will you do me the pleasure of picking them up with me?" asked one of the volunteers.

"Sure," I said.

"It's all set then. Layal and Maryam are going to pick them up and we'll specify and organize a room and supply them with water and food."

Maryam was the volunteer that picked me up from the airport. I had talked to her a lot but this was the first time that I'd known her name. She looked more European than Arab which is why I thought she was a foreign volunteer. Maryam always had a very calm expression that I had admired. How could she remain so calm working in emergency situations like this? I mean, it was only my first day and I had already started feeling the weight of the world on my shoulders.

"How's your first day? Everything alright?" asked the volunteer sitting next to me.

"Yeah, everything's good," I replied. The meeting came to an end and we were dismissed. I went to my room straight away and started working on my home school assignments. It was even more challenging to be homeschooled her as the Wi-Fi was very weak and I was extremely busy and exhausted all the time. I worked on my first assignment until darkness occupied the window across my desk. I was going to have my first field work experience tomorrow morning and so, I decided to have as much rest as I possibly could.

I woke up to the sound of Maryam knocking on my bedroom door, "ten minutes!", she shouted. I jolted up from my bed… we were leaving in ten minutes? I looked at the clock. 7:30 AM. It was way too early for me to wake up but I was on duty now and I knew I had to get up. I hurriedly got off my bed, washed my face, brushed my teeth and changed into casual jeans and a shirt. I was also given a volunteer vest which I wore for the first time with pride. The feeling I felt wearing that vest was exceptionally freeing. That itself, was worth all the pain I had previously felt. I quickly jogged into the car in the driveway and Maryam was already waiting for me there.

"You ready for your first assignment?" she asked.

"I'm more than ready," I enthusiastically replied. I felt more alive than ever; this is truly what I wanted to do for the rest of my life.

We drove out of the shelter area and into the main road. I hadn't seen so many israeli flags in such a long time and the view of the road made my blood boil once again. I engaged in small talk with Maryam in order to distract myself from this anger that I was furiously feeling.

"So what's new since I've been gone?" I asked.

"Well, nothing much. There's still a lot of raiding and attacking. Well, they have also created a sort of bomb that explodes within the human body and I have never seen anything crueler than that."

"What?" I asked, in shock, "a bomb that explodes within the body?"

"Yeah and it's exactly what it sounds like. The israeli soldiers throw it and it sticks to the person, slowly deteriorating and going off."

"Have you seen someone with that case?"

"Yeah, just a couple. Two or three people, I think. I saw a 15 year old boy going through it… I was with the shelter's paramedics and it was a first degree emergency, I saw gas leaving the boy's head and then I realize the gas was coming from a bomb," she took a deep breath, "there was nothing we could possibly do, if we touched him in the wrong place, it would have completely exploded and killed us all. We carried him and laid him down in a big puddle of water to loosen the effects of the bomb but it was a sure thing that he would've died from first impact."

"Do you see that often? People dying, I mean."

"Not as often as you'd expect but yeah, often… around 4-5 people a day, especially when houses are being bombed. A whole family, all together."

"Do you ever get used to it?"

"No. Never. The idea of death is and always will be a shocking thing, no matter how many times you witness it. Last month, I went on an assignment to a house on the Eastern side of the country and the people hadn't died yet, they were just in a lot of pain. A bomb was thrown in the house and it immediately went off but surprisingly, it didn't kill anyone. The house got bombarded which meant the walls broke down onto some of the people in the house and it led to broken bones which in return meant there was a lot of pain, crying and screaming. I thought we could save them, I really did. But as I was in the house, another bomb went off in a house right next to them and the people actually died out of fear. Do you know that people can actually die from an intense amount of fear? I just don't know how scared they were to have survived a bomb attack but die of another bomb's sound."

"Do the bombs scare you?"

"No, not really. I mean yeah, the aftermath scares me but the sound of the bomb is almost like the national anthem to me; I'm used to it. I was born and raised here after all."

"Did your house ever get bombed?"

"Yeah, I was fifteen when it happened. The house collapsed to the floor. My brother was killed. My parents immediately moved away with my sisters but I insisted on staying. I couldn't get myself to leave the land where I lost my brother in. He was my best friend. Do you have any siblings?"

"An elder brother and a little sister… they both passed away when israeli forces attacked my house."

"May God accept your tributes to him," she stopped talking and parked the car, "we're here."

I climbed out of the car and stood in front of the house. The house was entirely made from bricks, there was sand everywhere and the house didn't even have a door. This social class was even lower than mine. As I walked in, I noticed the natural sun light that the house had. I looked up to see a roofless house. My heart broke. Maryam and I were welcomed by a small family of 4: two parents and two children; a boy and a girl. Not only did the children look young, so did their parents.

"Are you guys ready?" Maryam asked them.

"Yeah, we've got everything that we need," replied the mom.

"Follow me into the car then." They followed Maryam and I into the car and I observed in awe the way Maryam knew exactly what to say to them and how to act. Her experience was evident through the way she handled the assignment. I was glad to be assigned to work by her side. She had a very lively personality. She constantly smiled and engaged in small talk not only with me, but also with the family we had just picked up.

Half way back to the shelter, we were stopped. Maryam stopped the car abruptly and rolled down her windows. We stood by the check point and two israeli soldiers were standing with their guns in their arms. A small flutter of fear made its way to my chest.

"Where are you going?" asked the soldier.

"A shelter at the other side of the municipality," replied Maryam very calmly.

"What do you need a shelter for, we've provided you with more than enough resources," said the soldier mockingly and let out a chuckle. Maryam stared at him in silence and I could feel the fear accumulate from the backseat where the family were seated.

"My joke isn't funny enough for you?" asked the soldier.

"Oh, I'm sorry… it was a joke? I didn't quiet catch it."

"Should we let them pass?" the soldier asked the other soldier standing next to him.

"Hmm… let's see," he paused and took a good look inside the car then pointed at me, "You! Get out of the car now."

I looked at Maryam and she signaled me to comply. I opened the door and got out of the vehicle. Maryam also got out and stood next to me.

"We've got a brave one," said one of the soldiers as he pointed at Maryam.

I could feel my heart race out of my chest. My heart was thumping so loud and my chest was moving so quickly that I had to wonder whether or not the soldiers saw it. The soldiers conducted a quick security check on us and then asked us to get back into the car.

"Drive safe and don't get yourselves into trouble ladies," the soldier mockingly said as he signaled us to move.

Maryam started the car and drove at a 100km/h. I was still shaking and in a state of complete fear. I hadn't been treated like a criminal in a very long time. I was physically unable to calm myself down.

"Are you okay?" Maryam asked.

I nodded quickly, unable to gather my breath and speak verbally.

"Hey… it's okay. Nothing happened. You're okay," she held my hand, trying to soothe me.

I took a deep breath. "It's her first time," Maryam said to the family sitting at the back seat.

"Honestly, it wasn't my first time and I was sitting in the backseat and I was afraid for my life," said the mother sitting behind me.

"It scares me every time but I'm starting to get used to it a bit. You will too," she looked at me then looked back at the road, "do you want to drink some water?"

"Yes," my voice was barely audible.

Maryam leaned to left hand side and grabbed a bottle of water and handed it to me. I slowly drank the water, feeling like air was finally making its way into my lungs. I felt much better. I breathed deeply for a couple of minutes to get myself back together.

"What are your names?" Maryam asked the family, trying to ease them.

"I'm Yousif and my wife is Fatima…" he stopped and pointed at his children, "that is Rami and my daughter is Nadia."

"Well, it's really nice to meet you."

We finally made it to the shelter. The family followed us inside but as soon as I walked in, the leader asked to speak to me.

"Are you okay?" she instantly asked.

"Yeah, I'm fine," I replied, "did Maryam tell you I got scared? I'm so sorry. I promise it won't happen again."

"No, she didn't tell me but everyone has a rough first day. Don't apologize for feeling fear… it's a normal human feeling, will you follow me to the office?"

I followed her into the office where she had a seat on the sofa and asked me to sit right across from her.

"So tell me… what happened today?" she asked warmly.

"Nothing," I replied. I didn't want her to have a negative first impression of me. I didn't want her to think of me as a coward or even worse, see me as the kid I really am.

"This is a judge free area… speak freely and trust me, it feels much better to speak about it."

And so, I slowly told her about the officers who stopped us and gave us a security check.

"I know it's nothing but I was just afraid at that moment."

"Do you feel better now?" she asked, "you're safe right here with us."

"I know… Maryam calmed me down… I instantly felt a lot better."

"Alright then let's go make sure our guests have everything they need."

I was amazed by the amount of work the volunteers had put in the room as soon as I walked in to it. The room used to be a store room and so it was really dusty and old but they had renovated it to the point where it almost looked like my room in Norway; spacious and gives a hopeful vibe.

I watched the little girl's eye glisten with joy as she ate ice cream and I realized how the small things really matter. We had provided them with basic everyday life necessities and I could already physically feel how they were exhilarated with joy; they were as happy as they'd probably be if they were on a vacation in Europe. I handed the little girl my iPad and showed her how to use it and play the games I had downloaded for her. I watched her as she played gleefully and chuckled from time to time. Her chuckles spread electric joy down my spine. I found myself subconsciously smiling and I was the happiest I've ever been in years.

I left the room, giving them some privacy and as I made my way into the reception area. I found more families coming in, I was surprised to find out that each of those families was given a temporary room here until electricity and water was back. I welcomed them all to the shelter and then made my way next to the door. I suddenly heard sirens. israeli police! By law, they had no right to demolish or attack a shelter so why were they coming our way? I ran back inside and called the leader.

"Police! Police!" I was shouting as if I had lost my mind.

"Stay behind," she calmly said and stood next to the door, waiting for the police to get out of their vehicle. I stood behind her and watched the police walk up to her with their big guns in their hands. I felt fear crippling in my heart. Is this what it's going to be like? A constant state of eternal fear?

"Do you have license for this shelter?" asked one of the soldiers as the other two stood by his side, holding their gun's in the leader's face. I really admired the way our shelter leader stood strongly like a mountain in front of them, unafraid by their weapons in her face.

"Yes, we do and it's supposed to be in your system, isn't it? So how about you check your database before coming to investigate with us?" she sharply spoke.

They started speaking in Hebrew and then the soldiers walked closely to her, their guns making physical contact to her forehead. She didn't even flinch. I had never been so impressed by someone. How could she be this brave?

"You better watch your tone," the soldier threatened her, "can we see the license?"

"Give me a minute."

"No!" shouted the soldier and then pointed at me, "get that girl to get it to you, you're staying here."

I looked up to her, waiting for her approval.

"Go in and ask Maryam for it," she calmly ordered me. I hurried into the shelter, looking for Maryam until I found her in the kitchen.

"The license… I need the license… shelter license… Police!"

Maryam held me by my shoulders and calmly spoke, "calm down and tell me what you need."

Her warm eyes warmed my heart up and my breathing went back to its normal pace.

"The police are at the door and they… want to see the shelter's license."

"Okay… it's not a problem, give me a minute."

I watched her as she calmly went into the meeting hall and came back in a few minutes with a piece of paper in her hands.

"Let's go?" she asked and I followed her to the door where the leader was standing with guns pointing to her face.

"Is this the license?" asked the soldier as he pointed at Maryam's hand.

Maryam handed him the license and he took a good luck at it and then threw it on the floor with sheer disrespect. He almost seemed disappointed that we actually had a permit for the shelter. I watched the guns slowly being moved from the leader's head to the air. They both pulled the trigger and shot at the air, clearly wanting to scare us. And they succeeded because I felt my heart drop to my stomach… Maryam immediately held my hand.

"It's fine," she whispered, "we're okay."

"You no longer have business in our shelter so please make your way back to wherever the hell you came from," said the leader.

The soldier hit her with the handle of his gun with a great amount of force; she immediately collapsed and he just gave out a laugh and walked away. Maryam and I sat next to her on the floor, she was conscious but in a lot of pain. I quickly ran inside the shelter and got ice packs to put on her forehead which had started swelling. I was shocked to still see her not expressing any sort of pain… I mean I was in pain just by looking at her. I kneeled down and touched the back of her forehead to check if there were any injuries, only to see my hands soaked with her blood. My heart started racing and the volume of blood making its way out of her body, made me dizzy. Maryam wrapped a cloth around her head in an attempt to stop the blood gushing out of her head. I called the paramedics and they quickly first aided her; they wrapped her head tighter than Maryam originally had and tried to get her to speak but it looked like she was already starting to lose her consciousness.

Chapter 13

"Can you hear me?" the paramedic loudly asked her. There was no response. Her pupils were dilated and her heart beat was starting to slow down. The paramedic quickly carried her into the car and drove away to the hospital, we were asked to stay in the shelter.

With fear still taking over my body, I sat down on the floor of the meeting hall and put my head into my palms. I felt the tears trickling down my cheeks. I felt someone's presence next to me and it was one of the other volunteers, she was also uncontrollably crying. I had only known the leader for a couple of hours yet I was so sad to see her hurt so how about the other volunteers who have been working with her for the last couple of years? Suddenly, someone came to the door and spoke, "quit the sobbing, this isn't what she would've wanted you to do. Get up and start taking care of our guests," said a man who looked look he was in his mid 30's, he was fairly dark skinned but his light eyes glimmered through the dark. His hair already had streaks of grey but I wasn't surprised, how could he not have grey hair after dealing with all this stress? It was only my first day but I wouldn't have been surprised if I found grey streaks in my hair already.

"Yes, it's enough girls… let's go," said another deep voice. I had seen the two men in the meeting but I had never interacted with them till now. I think one of them was the leader's husband but I was unsure of which one exactly. I carried my heavy body from the floor and followed them to a big room. The room had a lot of windows which was uncommon as we tended to lessen the amount of windows in the shelter so that the israeli occupation couldn't directly throw tear gas into the house. It also had a bright blue colored wall and wooden floors; it was very joyous and it looked more like a nursery room than anything else.

"We have three boxes over there and there are about 1000 food parcels. The food will be distributed in the shelter and we'll assign a specific team to distribute the left over parcels in the village, any volunteers?"

Instantly a couple of volunteers raised their hands. I didn't. I knew I talked a lot about engaging in field work and making a difference but I couldn't. I was tied and imprisoned by this fear that I was feeling. I knew things would be bad, but not to this point. I was here years ago and I suffered in prison but living in Norway made me forget the intensity of the pain I felt here and now I was back and I didn't know how to cope with it. I didn't want to be just another person who comes to help only to find themselves running away but I was afraid and I didn't think that there was anything I could do to overcome that fear.

"Layal, you're staying here?" asked Maryam, I could almost see the pity in her eyes and I hated it. They all referred to me as 'the kid' and even if they didn't intend it to be interpreted this way, I felt so helpless and so weak. Like a kid.

"Yeah… I don't feel well," I replied.

"It's alright, don't worry," she said, "wanna help me carry the boxes?"

"Sure," I replied. The boxes were a lot heavier than what they looked like; it took about four volunteers to carry each box. We carried the box to the other side of the room, next to the door, and cut it horizontally open. I emptied the boxes and placed the –really hot parcels, on the floor in order. The first boxes were taken to the families who were staying temporarily and then to the orphans. We were always taught to respect our guests which is why the families were the top priority. Maryam left with the rest of the team to distribute but I stayed inside the building. I was really worried about the leader… I made my way to my room and laid down on my bed. I prayed that she would recover quickly and that she'll be okay.

For the first time since I had arrived, I picked up my phone. I had a text. It was from Mohammed.

"How's everything?"

As soon as I read the text, I immediately gave him a call… after three rings, he picked up.

"I miss you," he quickly said.

"I miss you too."

"Are you okay? What's with your voice?"

"Yeah I'm just tired… it's been a stressful day."

"Wanna talk about it?" he asked.

"I'm okay," I said, "how's everything back in Norway?"

"Everything felt better the second I heard your voice… I wish you were here."

I heard him talk about his day for a good fifteen minutes until someone called out my name from across the hall… I felt like I was living in a movie. Time flew by and every second was so eventful. I felt all sorts of emotions in just one day; sadness, excitement, happiness, depression.

"I take it you have to go?" asked Mohammed.

"Yeah, I'm sorry." I hung up and quickly made my way across the hall.

I saw Maryam standing across the hall with all the volunteers; the place was crammed with people. Some were crying whilst others looked like they've turned emotionally numb. The 30 year old volunteer had his face in his palms and was sobbing and as I saw him, it sank; she passed away. I was also assured that he was her husband. The view of everyone completely broken down brought the same grief I felt when my family passed away back to my heart. Was it this easy to lose someone here or was I just completely unlucky to have someone pass away on the first day?

I quickly went to my room, starting to feel like I was a curse anywhere I went. I laid down on my bed and started to rethink everything that has happened since I arrived. I just wasn't sure if I could handle all of this on my own, it was too much. It was much more than I had anticipated. As I was flipping through the radio, trying to find something to distract me from the harsh reality of life, the little girl I talked to on the phone walked into my room.

"Is everything okay?" I asked as soon as I saw her.

"I need help with the art project," she innocently said, "I couldn't find the leader."

I swallowed my pain, trying as hard as I possibly could to not show her the intense amount of pain I was feeling in my chest. My chest was beating so quickly that it almost felt like my heart was banging itself onto the wall of my chest.

"What's the project? I might be able to help you."

She started explaining her project to me, "so basically, I want to draw Masjid Al-Aqsa because we were asked to draw something that has a special place in our heart. And well, my family and I used to spend every Friday in the Masjid so it's a representation of my family and just like I miss going to the mosque, I also miss my family."

She showed me her canvas. Her painting looked very impressive to me. It was perfect.

"What do you need help with? It's absolutely beautiful!"

"I'm trying to fit a small drawing of my family somewhere but I don't know where… they're a big part of this picture to me and I don't want the picture to seem incomplete."

"How about there?" I asked, pointing at an empty space.

"No, this is supposed to be where I'll draw the Palestinian flag…" she paused for a while, "can I draw them on the flag?"

"Yeah, why not? I'm sure it'll look amazing."

"Thank you so much," she said and walked out of my room.

This was the weird thing of volunteering for field work here; one minute I am depressed beyond words, the next, I'm so joyous that it almost feels like my heart's going to burst. Helping someone filled me with so much satisfaction that I wouldn't have wanted to be in any other place. I know I was helping people but something inside me said, is this enough? Is what I'm doing enough or am I just being too idealistic? Honestly, I found myself never having any answers to my questions.

I went to the meeting hall and saw all the volunteers gathered around as usual. Maryam signaled me to have a seat next to her.

"How are you holding up?" she asked.

"Mixed feelings but overall it's okay. How are you? I'm sorry for your loss," I said.

"She was like a sister to me, I mean, everyone here is like a sister to me. I'm going to miss her a lot but people come and go here… I know it's going to be okay. I'm used to this. We lose people all the time. As revolutionaries, we're willing to sacrifice as many people as it takes, in hopes that one day everything will be okay."

"What's your definition of things becoming okay?"

"I don't know. Being able to sleep without the fear of being attacked? Having access to water and electricity without the israeli forces turning it off suddenly? Not being afraid of spending time outside?"

"I don't think we'll ever get that. I hope we do but I just don't think so… at least not with the way the major countries in the world are acting… we don't have money which means no one's going to help us. What'd they get out of it? Nothing. Absolutely nothing."

"And you know what gets to me the most? Not that we are invaded. Not that we are constantly being killed. Not that I don't have any blood relatives alive. No. It's the fact that all of this is happening yet no one's talking about it. The fact that we can't do anything about it. That's the worst part. Not being able to do anything to change this."

"And they think donations are enough? I mean yeah, we're glad we get jackets in winter and so on, but that is not a permanent change. We want a change. A real one and that can only be done if powerful countries think justly and fight for our right. We're being stripped off our land while the people invading us are getting financial aid? What kind of logic is that?! I don't understand it and I don't think I ever will."

The late leader's husband called our attention.

"Can I get everyone's attention?" he asked and waited a couple of minutes for everyone to settle down and then he started speaking, "we are all very sorry for the loss of one of our most valuable team members. We are sad but this sadness cannot take a toll on us. Most of you know me, my name is Yousif and I closely worked with my wife in this shelter so I will be taking over leadership. I know it's a hard time but we must work together to overcome it. Millions are dying every day and we can't stop our work because we lost one of our members… there are people out there who depend on us. Anyways, to cut this meeting short, we have a lot of upcoming aid projects which we'll be planning very soon and just like before, if anyone of you has any kind of trouble, feel free to come see me. You all know which ones my room and you all have access to my phone number. Any questions?"

One of the volunteers raised her hand.

"Yes?" asked Yousif.

"Do you have a plan for tomorrow?"

"Well, we'll spend the morning right here in the shelter and then a team, of my choosing, will be coming with me to an elementary school where we'll provide free counselling to the children."

I prayed to get a place on that project; not because I wanted a change of scenery but because I have genuinely found that helping others is a therapeutic experience. I was one of the first people to leave the hall and make it back to my room. There was a sense of security that I felt within the walls of my room; it was the only place where I was truly able to express my emotions in.

Chapter 14

I checked my phone at the end of the day, only to see a text from Fairooz.

"Doing good?" it read.

"The whole experience is a rollercoaster of emotions but I think I'm doing fine so far," I replied.

I turned my phone off for the night. As I laid down, I felt as if I was sinking deeper than usual on the mattress... Yes, I did feel like I was weighed down by all the pain I've felt in just one day but it did really physically weigh me down? Everything was too much and in that moment, I just wanted to close my eyes and wake up in a country that is safe, more specifically, in a safe Palestine. Sleep overcame me quickly. I've noticed it's been easier for me to sleep here... I don't know if it was because I was finally home or because every day is so eventful that by the time I get into my bed, I'm exhausted.

I was woken up early morning by my alarm clock. It almost felt like I was back in school. I sleepily made my way to the bathroom and got ready for what I hoped would be a better day than yesterday. I immediately made my way to the meeting hall and waited for all the volunteers to arrive. Yousif walked in, 15 minutes late, he had bloodshot eyes and his face had started turning pale. I guess his wife's death had just sunk in his mind. I overheard Maryam telling him to take a break but he refused, saying it was his duty to continue what his wife had started. The way Yousif looked had brought an intense feeling of sadness in my already weak heart. Yousif was usually the most cheerful volunteer, he was the only one who'd smile in our morning meetings but today, even he was down. It's weird how we don't have much empathy for people who are often upset and negative than those who are typically found to be happy and positive and then face a sudden break down.

"Okay everyone, please stay quiet as my voice is a bit low today," the hall instantly went silent, "Maryam, Husam, Layal and Jameel are going to be at the elementary school today with me, Ahmed and his group will take charge of the shelter here and all the rest will follow his lead. Today is not supposed to be a very eventful day... there are no warnings of any attacks but you never know so please try to keep everyone as safe and as close to the hiding spot as possible. Any questions?"

"What time are we leaving for the elementary school?" asked one of the men.

"In about 20 minutes," Yousif replied.

The three volunteers and I all made our way to our rooms to get ready and packed for the day. I didn't know what to expect... I've never done counselling. To be completely honest, I didn't even know why Yousif had chosen me, I had no experience and was pretty much still a child. I packed as much food as I possibly could in my backpack because I knew it was something the children there pretty much lacked. Life is hard here. It really is. And to them, I've had it easy. As soon as I was ready, I sat in the reception area alongside Maryam, waiting for the others to get ready.

"Have you done this before?" I asked Maryam.

"Yes and no... I've done it with teenagers. It's very interesting, you'll like it."

"I don't know what to do... I don't even know why Yousif chose me."

"You have a strong background... most of the volunteers here are from more upper class backgrounds and never experienced what you and many others have. You'll be able to relate so trust me, it will come naturally to you."

She kind of eased my mind, "did you enjoy it when you counselled teenagers? How is it exactly?" I asked.

"Yeah, I loved it. I got to know a lot about many people's experiences and you'll notice how they start speaking with a very negative mindset and then slowly, it becomes more and more positive. It's very intriguing how their mindset changes quickly. You'll leave feeling so much better, trust me."

The boys slowly started arriving one by one.

"Is everyone ready?" Yousif asked. He looked so much better than he did in the morning; his hair was styled neatly and he looked like he had more color in him. He was almost smiling. "Alright then, let's go," he enthusiastically said.

We followed him into a car and I had a seat next to Maryam. Yousif was sitting on my other side and it made me really happy because I had a lot to talk to him about. Jameel drove the car and Husam was in the passenger's seat.

"Are you excited?" Yousif asked me.

"I don't know," I replied, "I've never done anything like this before. I don't know what to expect."

"You'll love it," he said.

"Have you done something like this before?"

"Yes, I have and with all age groups. I've been working in this shelter for ten years so I've been here since the very beginning. I counselled Husam when he was in high school, tell her about it."

"Yeah, it's true," Husam said, "He counselled me in high school and I was going through a lot, I lost many of my loved ones and it was really hard, I came to work with the shelter as soon as I graduated from university."

"Did you find his counselling of much use?" I asked.

"Yeah, it's the reason why I am who I am today."

We never really realize how much impact small things have on the lives of others and personally, I think that's why, as a society, we're never going to get better. Everyone seems to be doing things to please themselves without putting others into consideration. It is completely fine to do things to make yourself happy but never when it means you'd have to compromise on someone else's happiness. This has always been a rule that I live by. If you want to know whether what you're doing is right or wrong, then just see how people around you feel about it and no, on the contrary, this in no way means that you're living for others.

You are living for yourself but life is not a one man's game; we have to coexist together to make it work.

"Jameel has done counselling too last year, right?"

"Yeah," he replied from behind the wheel.

"How was your experience?"

"To be honest, I never really got to connect with the kids. It wasn't as good as I expected it to be."

"Then why did you agree to try it again?"

"I don't know. I guess just because you have one bad experience doesn't mean you should never try again."

"Have you done any voluntary work abroad?" I asked.

"No not really, we've got a lot going on here," replied Yousif.

"But what makes Palestine more worthy than the other countries? I mean Yemen is having the worst famine outbreak in history, don't they deserve some help too? I mean, I feel like every country should have an equal chance of being helped."

"You do have a point but what you're saying is too idealistic. I mean, I wish we could help people from everywhere but sadly, it's not humanly possible. For now, we have decided to stick to people of our own country and then maybe if things get better, we could conduct voluntary work elsewhere."

"Have you always wanted to partake in voluntary work?" I asked him.

"Actually, I never thought about it before I met my wife, went to university and majored in Economics… I wanted to work in a bank but life had other plans for me, I guess."

"Do you ever regret this?"

"Sometimes… I wanted to work abroad so I know I would have been more comfortable there, and possibly still married, but I don't know.

Overall, I do feel good working here too. I studied in New Zealand so I always figured that I'd just get a job there. I settled and all but my wife had other plans. Now, I'm used to this, I can't imagine living or working elsewhere. I think Maryam also studied abroad, didn't you?"

"No, I didn't have the opportunity to do so. I went to a university here and I majored in communication but wasn't really able to get a job. I was offered one here and I took it. I never imagined this life for myself but I wouldn't replace it now with anything else."

"Not a lot of us get the opportunity to study abroad, I was offered a scholarship a really long time ago but we don't have those anymore and money is just tight. By the way, how's your home school going? I was asked to follow up with that."

"It's doing fine," I mumbled.

"Really?

"Yeah, I'm just finding it difficult to balance school work with voluntary work… by the time I'm back home, I'm way too tired to do anything."

"You should've said something before-hand, I'll arrange your schedule to not be too hectic and allow you enough time to get your work done, alright?"

"Yeah that sounds good, thank you."

"Alright, we're here," Jameel said as he stopped the car.

The school was broken down… it had a very small cottage like structure and seemed to barely have space to fit us, let alone the children. We walked into the school, following Yousif's lead. The children glimmered with happiness as soon as they saw us because when they saw visitors, they knew that food would be available. The school's principal told us that they rarely ever had enough food to fill all the students, so each student had to eat a very small amount every day so that all 60 students can eat on a daily basis. One of the children, immediately caught my eyes. Her skin was dark from the sun she has been sitting under every single day but her bright eyes glowed with a vibrant green color. Despite the vibrancy of her eyes, I could still see the sadness that was embedded deep within. It spoke to me. I looked at her and felt an intense aura of love come over me. It was as if I had met someone who I knew in the other world.

"Hi," I said, speaking to her, "what's your name?"

"Sara," she shyly said.

"It's really nice to meet you, I'm Layal. She shyly smiled as I sat down on the floor in front of her.

"How is school?" I asked her, trying to initiate a conversation.

"I was very upset when I saw that my school had been damaged but now I'm very glad to be back."

"What happened to your school?"

"I don't know…" she took a pause and continued, "one day I came here and I saw that the school was really damaged, there walls were all teared down and I saw a lot of bullet remains and rubble on the floor. I don't know what happened but we couldn't come to school anymore and instead, we met every day in caravans and temporary shelters to continue learning; it wasn't even half as effective as we had over 50 students in a single caravan. I hated going to school after that although school was the best part of my life before but now, I'm very happy to be back again."

"You've always been in this school?"

"No, I was in a school in East Jerusalem until the israeli occupation built a wall and separated the two areas… I wasn't allowed in East Jerusalem after that and even if I tried to walk there, my previous 10 minute walk had turned into a full one hour journey and I had to climb walls and fences to get there so my parents decided it wasn't safe enough."

"You know I went to school not too far from here and it looked exactly like this school so this makes me feel very nostalgic. I can't help but look back at all the friends I had, have you made friends already?"

"Yeah," she pointed at a group of girls on the other side of the field, "they're my friends."

"Don't they want to come hang with us? Call them."

I watched her run to the other side of the field and talk to them.

"How's it going?" I suddenly heard Maryam ask.

"I feel free… does it make sense? I feel free. That's the only word I have to describe it."

"I know how it feels. Enjoy it as it lasts," she said and disappeared.

I watched the little girls run all the way back to me.

"Hey," I said, "so I know Sara but I don't know you girls, who's who?"

"That's Zeina," she pointed at the girl on the right, "and the other one's Rana… they're my best friends…"

I remembered having best friends… those days were long gone. I wasn't even friends with one person who I used to be with in school. It wasn't as sad as I expected it to be, I mean, I used to think that drifting away from my best friends would be so hard, that I couldn't live without them, but I moved on pretty quickly. That was when I realized that school friends were really just temporary, at least, to me. I came back to reality and listened to the girls as they told me about their lives. Apparently, Rana aspired to be a doctor, a career that would be particularly difficult for her to achieve since she comes from a very small village and a family that are well below the poverty line. I remember being their age and thinking that everything was possible but with them, it seemed like they really understood everything. Rana knew for a fact that her dream wasn't very achievable and she knew exactly why. What impressed me about her was the fact that although she knew she'd probably never be able to be a doctor, it didn't stop her from working hard. She was the top scorer in her whole batch which was very impressive considering there were A LOT of students in that school. Zeina was a bit less academic but still ambitious… she wanted to be a journalist; it was interesting how her parents were both journalists, her father was a martyr; he was killed on the job, but her mom continues to be a journalist. She spoke a lot about how women were less likely to be on media but her mother defied that and she hopes to do the same as well. I was impressed by the amount of intellect those little girls had. I guess it was true that going through many hardships leads the individual to grow faster. Although the girls were in fourth grade, to me, they spoke at a level of intelligence and intellectuality that I probably still didn't have. When Maryam told me that I'd learn a lot from the children, I thought she was saying it metaphorically but in fact, I felt like I gained more from this experience than the children themselves. It made me very happy to see the future generations of my country; they were much more intelligent and ambitious than we ever were. Back in Norway, children were children, they played and they were completely stress free but here, I could see the amount of experience and pain from the children's eyes. They carried much more words than what they expressed. In a way, I felt as though even if they spoke for years on top of years, they'd never be able to empty the amount of words they have buried deep down their hearts.

As the sun had started setting, we started making our way back to the shelter. As volunteers, it was easier for us than it was for them. We had immunity and although the israeli government forgot about it most times and did attack us every so often, we were still in a much better situation than them. We had somewhere to go back to at the end of the day, they didn't.

As we headed back home, I laid down on my bed and reassessed everything going on. We were occupied. As an important country in the Muslim community, we had a lot of other countries that claimed to support us but the reality was, no one really did. Everyone just supported us when it was convenient to them. The support we got from rich Arab countries was so limited that we could almost say it was nonexistent. I was unsure of a lot of things in my life but I was sure of one very important thing: one day, the whole world will realize that israel has successfully controlled all the Arab nations in the world but is still fighting to control our Palestine.

<u>Author's Note:</u>

I've always wondered why the israeli-Palestinian occupation has dragged on for so long and why the world has been so quiet about it; I found the answer to that the day I decided to write this book. See as human beings we are made to be selfish, we always think of ourselves before thinking about other which is why talking about this conflict between ourselves is easy but talking about it to the world is a very hard task to do. When I first had the idea of writing this book, the first thing that came to my mind was: am I willing to take this risk? And you might think what risk would a 17-year-old be taking when talking about such conflict. Well, the first thing I thought about was I've always dreamt of studying abroad so what if the person in charge of the admissions was pro-israel, there would be a bias towards me and it was then that I realized how selfish we humans are; there are people dying and I'm thinking about such silly thing. And it was in that moment that I said to myself; I have to do this. We no longer have the time to be thinking about our own agenda, the world is a mess. It's time to wake up.

It is no secret that the israeli occupation has occupied multiple parts of Palestine, more specifically: The West Bank including East Jerusalem and the Gaza Strip, this also includes one of the most holy mosques in Islam: Masjid Al-Aqsa. Not only have the israeli forces occupied important parts in the country but they have continued to break human rights laws by evicting Palestinian civilians and demolishing their houses, arrests, ill-treatment of civilians, using weapons and lethal gasses to subdue nonviolent protests, torture of prisoners and the list of human rights violations by israeli forces goes on and on. These violations have not only harmed the Palestinians but also the israeli citizens who have to live and witness all these inhumane acts and bear the results of violence in the region.

But who am I to speak about something I have never experienced… So don't take my word for it, the words of thousands of Palestinians who have suffered under the israeli Occupation.